'This absolutely stunning, wonderfully observed novel challenges all preconceived ideas about supposedly "ordinary" lives' *The Times*

'A sweet, bitter, wonderfully told tale' *Daily Mirror*

'A grimly poignant tale of youthful rebellion and small-town romance ... Barton manages to create something out of the ordinary from the mire of "newspaper ink, Coty lipstick and canine grease" which characterises these seemingly nondescript lives' *Guardian*

'Delightfully bracing ... as a sweet, thoughtful debut it leads you around the rain-sodden houses, paints you a portrait, before sending you away with a sullen kiss' *Independent on Sunday*

'A charming and irresistible story of how marriage and family life are stifling yet deeply comforting' *Psychologies*

'Lovely, descriptive prose ... Barton's conversational style had me reading this book easily in two sittings' *thebookbag.co.uk*

'[A] promising first novel ... excellent ... Wonderful writing' *Independent*

'Barton's poetic prose ensures that although the story is set during 1994, there's a timeless quality to the story, as if the town's inhabitants have been frozen in time in a Lowry painting ... Her delicate depiction of characters creates a real sense of intrigue regarding this seemingly doomed relationship' *Big Issue*

'Nostalgic, sad and beautifully w

Laura Barton was born in Lancashire in 1977, and now lives in London. She has been a journalist at the *Guardian*, and has also written for Q, the *Word*, *Intelligent Life* and Radio 4. *Twenty-One Locks* is her first novel.

LAURA BARTON
TWENTY-ONE LOCKS

Quercus

First published in Great Britain in 2010 by Quercus
This paperback edition first published in 2011 by

Quercus
21 Bloomsbury Square
London
WC1A 2NS

A CIP catalogue record for this book is available
from the British Library

ISBN 978 0 85738 121 7

Printed and bound in Great Britain by Clays Ltd, St Ives plc

10 9 8 7 6 5 4 3 2 1

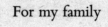
For my family

CHAPTER ONE

Wednesday, mid-February, and the scent of floor polish rises up through Pemberton's department store. Outside, a vague drizzle hangs over the town. Thin, grimy rain floats down on to the rooftops of King Street and Poolstock Lane, filling the gutters along Wallgate and Bridgeman Terrace and turning the pavements greasy. Above the chimney pots and the television aerials the sky looks bleary and unshaven. 'Another five minutes,' it seems to say, 'another five minutes, and then I will wake up.'

Shoppers flurry in from the rain-slicked streets, flapping their umbrellas into bony carcasses, checking the rumple and set of their hair. They drift down the escalator like slowly settling silt: brassy-haired girls shoe-shopping on their lunch-breaks; weasel-faced men, hands thrust deep into cheap jacket pockets; broad-hipped women in dust-coloured anoraks, lugging plastic carrier bags and killing time before the bus ride home. Light speckles of rain cling to their coats, linger on their hair and their pale, round faces, as they sink quietly into the perfume hall.

Below the St Emmanuelle counter the air hangs idle, heavy with the scent of cold cream and dust. There is the distant spritzing of perfume, the low burr of conversation, the jovial song of the lift. The ceiling lights beat down warmly, and beyond the blue eau de cologne bottles clouds of old ladies drift by with cumulus hair. Down here in the heat and the dust, Jeannie sits on her haunches, brushing varnish on to a ladder in her tights and counting down the minutes until lunch. There are stains on her blouse and her nails are chipped. This morning, like all mornings, she left the house with wet hair.

She is pretty, in a mousy way, but there is something ditchwatery about her appearance: the sullen hue to her skin, the dreary colour of her thin hair. Her eyes are sallow, her cheeks caved, her chest sunken. It is as if she has been crumpled in the middle, like a cheap, hollow Easter egg. It is not an unusual look in this town, where the women are faded and creased and well-worn, but in the perfume hall at Pemberton's it is almost unprecedented. Among the swan-necked bottles of scent and the buxom jars of face cream and the lipsticks all lined up like chorus girls, Jeannie stands out like a blemish: slouching, most days, behind the counter, tugging at her fingernails and chewing at her lip like a piece of gristle.

The other perfume girls are exotic creatures, bronzed and highlighted and scarlet-nailed, their eyelids heavy with extravagant plumes of cerise and cerulean blue. A visit to the perfume hall of Pemberton's, therefore, is much like a tour of the parakeet house, alive with much fluttering and squawking and preening and fussing.

Each morning, one or other of these women will turn her tight, beady eyes towards Jeannie's cowering frame, and with a certain vulturine grace swoop across the hall, seize her by the collar and drag her up and away to the treatment rooms. Here she will smear her face with foundation and rouge, paint her lips Moroccan Rose and daub her eyes Sweet Almond. Well-manicured hands will wrench her thin, drab hair and twist it – as if wringing out a dishcloth – into a tight chignon. 'There,' she will announce with cold satisfaction, holding up a shaving mirror so that Jeannie might see her face, large and distorted and orange. 'Isn't that better?'

Quite how anyone of such terraced ordinariness became a perfume girl is a subject of some conjecture in the staff cafeteria at Pemberton's. The truth is that Jeannie, recently departed from the local technical college, found herself in the job centre on the very day that Nadine, the counter's previous incumbent, had run away with a cruise-ship dancer. It had begun as a temporary measure for both parties – the department store requiring an able body; Jeannie, somewhat adrift and in need of a short-term mooring. But now she has been here two years. And it seems to her sometimes as if the days have sailed by and she has done little more than stand waving from the shore.

Two years have changed the town little. The days still begin with the same sigh of the milk float, the first rain on the bedroom window, the grey walk along Atherton Road to the bus stop. The week still ends in the rubble of Saturday night, the drunkenness, the fights, the last bus home. And the year ebbs slowly, its seasons arriving cautioned by damp: spring, a sparring of tight-fisted buds and wet earth; summer little more than a short burst of rose queens, bonny baby contests, visiting circuses and weddings. The want of sunshine is met with hair bleach and bronzer, and the journey to town blurs by in a straggle of tanning salons and travel agents.

It is four months until Jeannie will be married. Viewed from this distance, her wedding seems a thing that is at once very near and very far away, like an object sitting at the bottom of the swimming pool. Yet there is a church booked and a dress chosen, and on her finger sits a diamond ring, bought from the jeweller in small, neat instalments.

As the months have passed since her engagement was announced in the local paper, as her nights have been filled with thoughts of hymns and royal icing and napkins folded like swans, she has found increasing comfort in the ordered world of Pemberton's. A glaze of calm stretches across its five floors, from haberdashery to homeware, menswear to millinery, and here, especially, in the perfume hall, where the piped music mingles with the scent of white musk and narcissus, and light bounces gaily off the glass bottles and the counter-tops.

Jeannie has learned a great deal during her two years in Pemberton's perfume hall. She has mastered the routine of cleansing, toning, moisturising. She has acquainted herself with the armoury of tweezers, brushes, sponges and eyelash curlers that lie in the narrow drawers beneath the counter. She has learned that blusher must sit on the apples of the cheeks, that a perfume has a head, a heart and a base, that it must be dabbed on the wrist, the throat, the breasts.

Nail polish dry, clock edging towards midday, she hauls herself awkwardly upright, dimly aware that one of her feet has gone to sleep, and for want of anything else to do, she stands scrunching her hand in the jar of tiny cotton-wool balls that sits on the glass counter-top and watches the customers descending the escalator. Increasingly, she has the gnawing feeling of merely filling time. There were, of course, many other things she might have done rather than work at Pemberton's: a BTEC in photography, perhaps, or night shifts packing at the ice cream factory. But they were all essentially serving the same purpose: just ways to fill the hours until something happened. Somehow, though, nothing ever did actually happen, and somehow she went nowhere, and like everybody else around here, just rolled back down, like a trickle of condensation.

This is an oxbow lake of a town. The industry died a decade ago, when the mills finally stuttered to a halt, the pits wound down and the borough slumped, tired and sullen and dejected, until it became a place it was easy to drift past – a railway station en route to the Lake District, an exit on the M58. Once, the town hummed with activity, and the air above ground danced with white cotton dust and the men emerged from the earth blackened with coal. Now everything is an unremitting grey. And yet there still remains a pride, tethered mostly to football and rugby and drinking, and in the park they still plant out the county seal in petunias, but they boarded up the bandstand and the tea rooms sit empty.

Jeannie was born in the August of 1972, on the very day the Leeds–Liverpool canal retired from working life. A short-boat named *Roland*, which lugged coal to the Westwood Power Station, made its final journey along its banks as, red-faced and squalling, Jeannie came into the world on the ninth floor of the local maternity hospital, housed in an old soap factory.

These days the canal is the preserve of pleasure-cruisers, Sunday walkers, glue-sniffers. It is where people drown puppies, where gangs of teenagers come to throw stones and drink beer. In the early mornings and on Sunday afternoons, men come to sit mutely on its banks and fish: barbel, bleak, gudgeon. In the summer months, schoolchildren make trips to the canal to spot coots and sticklebacks, and to trace their fingers along the smooth, deep scars in its stone bridges, grooves worn by the strong, thick ropes with which the horses dragged along the coal barges.

The canal is overgrown now, the trees have converged, the bridges hunched, and the water sits silent and dark. It is as if the land has chosen to close over the wound, and the canal now runs like an old, paling scar, 127 miles long across the North. Walking along its quiet banks, you forget the violent act that made it; the broken men riving the land, the sweat, the dirt, the lives lost.

This is a region that has been hacked at, cleaved, meddled with, and finally then left to rest. Occasionally now the land will shift slightly, as a restless sleeper turns in the night and kicks off his covers. The ground will yawn, old mine shafts gape open, the earth buckle and give way. And so the people who live here walk with a characteristic gait: shoulders raised, heads bowed, cowering from the rain, taking each step cautiously, as if both the sky might fall in and the ground might collapse beneath them.

It is a town famed as both a battleground and dance floor. Even today, the people are fighters and dancers. In the old days they danced in their clogs, the uppers cowhide and the soles alder, dancing heel and toe, the sound of their shoes echoing the rattle of the mill's loom and shuttle. They fought on the street corners, on the pit brow, and they fought on the canal boats, too. The miners fought liquored-up and naked but for their clogs. They called it purring. And if their opponent fell to the ground they'd throttle him. Then kick him in the head. They are still fighting. Late night and drunkenly. Though they use fists and bottles and knives these days. There are eighty-six pubs, four nightclubs, six kebab shops in the town, and these are the battlegrounds now for scuffles that invariably end in smashed windows, broken noses and the casualty department of the local hospital.

And when the weekends are over they return to the factories churning out ice cream and chutney and toffees, to the gasworks and the council, to shop jobs and building sites, to the waterboard and the electric and the burger bar. Many of them work at the factory that sits up on a hill on the outskirts of town and makes over forty varieties of tinned soup. They say that on some mornings the streets nearby smell of Scotch broth.

From the top of this hill you can watch the town unfold each day, the pale-faced factory workers leaving the night shift, the elderly who find themselves rising earlier and earlier these days, the school buses winding their way past the houses, pausing by street corners and postboxes to collect the children in their uniforms of grey or maroon or bottle-green. And there come the dog-walkers, the paper boys, the postmen, the businessfolk with their black leather briefcases, the women with prams, the pensioners, the dole-claimers, all going about their business, popping into newsagents, dropping by the bakery, boarding buses into town. And from somewhere far away comes the call of a funeral bell.

Between the bus station and the shopping arcade, the market hall stands soaked in dreary light, as if full of lives lived at a low wattage. It offers scrag-ends and cheap meat, factory seconds, shop-soiled dresses, dented cans and synthetic romance: nylon négligées, flocked cards and plastic flowers. And though it is always bustling with loud voices and brazen colours, big bodies and strong scents, to walk among its stalls is as if to find oneself inside an enormous jacket pocket, among all the fluff and the bus tickets, the small change and the scraps of tissue.

Up off the market runs the Royal Arcade, a modernised Victorian walkway full of chemists and bakeries and hair-dressing salons. The light floods through the glass roof, folds itself into the smell of hot pies. And the *Evening Post* vendor throws his call up into the air like a dove, to circle and swoop the length of the arcade, trying to escape.

At the top of the arcade there is a brief gulp of fresh, wet air. Across the street, the sliding doors of the new shopping complex slop open and shut, revealing a glimpse of its shopfronts and walkways. The complex arrived three years ago, in a flurry of beige-bricked optimism and much fanfare, but now most of its retail spaces sit empty.

Pemberton's opened its doors in 1928, specialising in fine furniture, porcelain, woollens and rainwear. The town had money then, and aspirations; people bought hats just for Sunday and crockery for best. Its founder, Arnold Pemberton, was a large and benevolent man with ruddy cheeks and a small, wet mouth. He had learned his trade on the family market stall, selling bric-à-brac, delivering furniture on an open cart and clearing dead men's houses. He was devoted to his department store, patrolling its floors each day with a sense of wonder, and there was an air of polish about him as he passed by, his bald head shining as brightly as his black leather shoes. But he was cursed by a wife who was small and bitter as a lemon-drop, and six children all of whom gambled and drank and sailed right off the rails. He retired in 1974, and the department store fell through their hands like an apple through branches, before finally landing in the safe, diligent grasp of his nephew. When Arnold died, aged 102, in a nursing home in Shevington Moor, no one had visited him in months. They found him in the day room, his orange squash undrunk and his *Evening Post* unread on the table beside him.

Pemberton's is built of a pale grey stone that once stood crisp and proud and immaculate. Dirt has settled in its crevices now, bringing to the building a saggy, wrinkled appearance, like elephant hide. Though most shoppers drift somewhat unceremoniously into the store via the shopping complex, the old façade still looks out on to the main street, all brass and plate glass and haughty-faced mannequins. Pigeons cluster on the window ledges, their eyes pink-rimmed and nervous, their feathers the same dirty grey as the masonry, and halfway up the building hangs a gilt-edged clock, its black hands sitting for ever at twenty to two.

The role of a Pemberton's perfume girl begins each morning at nine o'clock, at the staff entrance around the back of the store, a faded red metal door into which someone has scratched the words 'Shelley is a slag'. The day runs until half past five when the front doors are locked and the grilles pulled down for the night. To Jeannie, the hours in between are to be waded through, the day rising up to her middle like a puddle. There is a lunchbreak, an hour most often passed in the glower of the staff canteen or straying idly through town. Sometimes she will sit in the bus station café, and return to the perfume counter smelling of bacon fat. Or she will head to the railway station and stand on the platform with a cup of tea, watching the trains roll out.

She is always late back. The store manager, Mr Bridden, a man whose pale skin puts one in mind of uncooked meat, will glance at his watch and tut as Jeannie slinks into the building and hurries along the yellow staff corridors, slamming her locker door shut, reapplying her lipstick and darting back out on to the floor. 'It'll be coming off your wages!' he always calls after her. But it never does.

Kiki St Emmanuelle was a former beauty queen from a small town in north-west Ohio. She was born the more prosaic Katherine Grubb, the only girl in a family of corn-farming Grubbs. In 1924, having reigned variously as Miss Ohio Charm, Miss Corn Queen, and Miss Potato Blossom, she changed her name to St Emmanuelle, and put it to a small beauty parlour in her home town, selling perfumes, rouges, ointments and salves. With time, and perseverance, the St Emmanuelle name spread throughout America, sold first in Midwestern salons and drugstores, and later in the nation's department stores before establishing a foothold in Europe. The company's most famous product remains its signature scent, Kiki – a heavy floral of amber and orris and tuberose, sold in a voluptuous bottle of prussian-blue glass. In 1955 it sold four million bottles, and was the best-selling perfume in America.

There is a picture of Kiki Grubb inside the St Emmanuelle perfume counter manual. Jeannie will look at it sometimes: the thick blonde hair set back from her face in waves, and eyebrows drawn into fine, black arcs. She has farm-girl limbs, big and robust, the kind of sturdy frame that all the tailoring in the world – the jacket nipped at the waist, the blouses frilled at the collar – cannot truly feminise. She was, by all reports, not a pleasant woman; quick-tempered and self-important. Following her marriage to a wealthy New York banker, she severed all ties with her family back home in Ohio, and never returned to the small town that raised her.

There are seven St Emmanuelle fragrances now, each with its own family of talcum powders and body lotions, soaps and bath oils. But nobody buys much perfume from Jeannie's counter – unless it is Christmas, or Mother's Day, or there is a free gift promotion. On Saturdays, they buy moisturiser and nail varnish. But mid-week it is quiet, a few sales a day, and the perfume sits trembling in its bottles as the shoppers roll by, heading for the top-floor cafeteria.

There are seasonal promotions, special offers, giveaways, limited edition gift sets, and at such times Jeannie is required to stand smiling at the foot of the escalator with a bottle of scent, spraying the upturned wrists of passers-by. Standing there in navy-blue court shoes, waiting for people to come, an ache spreads from the toes to the ankles, to the calves and the knees, runs across the hips, up the spine to the shoulders. But there she must stand. Smiling and spritzing, smiling and spritzing. Wishing she were back behind the counter where she could slump quietly against the cupboards and daydream.

She has a friend up in haberdashery, a girl from school who will drift over when trade is slow, rest her freckled arms on the counter-top and chatter. But most of the time she listens to the other perfume girls, to Michaela and Kimberley and Nicola, as they discuss diets and shoes and hair and soap operas, and all the things they drank, all the men they shagged, on Friday night. She takes off her court shoes so she can concentrate, stands flat-footed behind the counter so the toes of her tights grow cool and dusty, and pictures them, wild on Bacardi, canoodling in the shadows of the churchyard.

When the grilles shudder down she dashes through the wet night and the arcade and the market hall to the bus station, and the number fourteen home. She sits at the back of the bus, head juddering against the window-pane, breathing in the musky scent of her jacket. Outside the rush-hour traffic drags by, slow and miserable, as a long hem through wet streets. A woman stands in the window of her front room, watching the road; behind her a television screen flickers brightly with the local news. Jeannie counts down the stops, listens to the death rattle of the bus doors. On Atherton Road, one by one, the streetlights are turning a soft fluorescent pink.

CHAPTER TWO

Her grandmother was boiling cauliflower, the room full of its sweet, watery smell and steam that bloomed white across the windowpane. The kitchen overlooked the back garden, with its coalhouse and rosebushes and its high brick walls; today the wind was wild, and the washing on the line was bucking and rearing like horses in a paddock.

Jeannie would often spend Sunday afternoons here as a child, sitting at the table reading comics, standing at the draining-board making perfume: a jam-jar stuffed with rose petals that she prodded until they grew twisted and grubby and damp as scraggy tissues. It never smelled of anything more than a wet, grey garden.

It would be years until she learned how perfume is

really made, not in jam-jars on draining-boards, not with tapwater and teaspoons. The traditional method of perfumery relies upon the process of distillation. Tall metal stills filled with fresh flowers, and water, five times their weight, poured in on top. In the great belly of the still, the flowers mulch, and their petals crumple, their colours run the bruised pink of a child's knees. And as the petals welter and wane, the still is heated, and up rises a flowery steam that flows all along the still's long neck, until it cools and condenses, drip-dripping into an oily essence.

This is much how love works in a small town; the sky and the walls and the familiarity of these streets holding these young hearts like a still. All this rain washes them together, their colours running, their lives mulching, till the warm, musky fumes of love swirl up. Jeannie has known Jimmy since infant school. They grew up on parallel streets, they played in the same park, they hung around in the same bus shelters, their lives crumpling together in a rainy town.

'Are you sure you won't stop for your tea?' Her grand-mother turns down the gas. 'There's plenty.' She is a broad woman, her bulk somewhat lessened by age, but still in possession of an air of immovability. Only once has this faltered, when Jeannie saw her standing in the bathroom wearing just her slip and girdle and no false teeth; she looked so small and frail, like a shelled walnut.

She catches glimpses of that vulnerability now, in her grandmother's crepey skin and feathery breath, in her appeals for her to stay just a little longer.

'No, thanks, Nan. Jimmy's cooking.' Jeannie pulls on her coat. 'I was just popping round those samples.'

'You've got him well trained!' Her grandmother squints at the small sachets of foam bath she has brought. 'What's this? Lily of the Valley? Very fancy!'

The local paper sits open on the table, and her grandmother has circled the death notices of all the people she used to know.

'Who's gone this week?' Jeannie asks as she unfolds her gloves.

'No one I liked,' her grandmother laughs, then leans in close to kiss her, and she smells sweet, of talcum powder and sugary tea.

Jeannie fishes out her Yale key and opens the front door. The hallway is limp with the smell of sausage fat and from the kitchen she can hear the radio blaring out a football match.

'You're late!' Jimmy bellows. He holds his hand in mid-air to quiet her. 'GO ON YER BASTARD!' he roars at the radio, and as the crowd sighs with disappointment at the goal missed he shakes his head. 'Daft sod,' he mutters.

She stands in the living room and unzips her coat while

the cheering wreaths around her. 'Sorry, love,' he says, and pecks her on the cheek. 'How was it at the coalface?'

'Oh fine,' she says, stepping out of her court shoes and scrunching her toes. 'Fine. What kind of trouble did you get up to?'

He is back in the kitchen now in his grubby blue T-shirt and his overalls rolled down to the waist, doling out sausages and mash and spilling gravy on the work surface. 'Christ on a bike, you wouldn't believe today!' he says, and he is off, talking about vans and carburettors, Fiestas and faulty gearboxes.

Jeannie sets the table, lining up the knives and forks with the pattern of the gingham cloth. She moves the fruit bowl, fetches the cruet, brushes the morning's toast crumbs into the palm of her hand. Jimmy sways through with the plates. '*Voilà!*' he says. 'Tuck in!' He has turned down the radio so that it makes a persistent buzzing sound, like a bluebottle in a jam-jar, and with one ear on the football he continues with his stories from the garage. 'You wouldn't believe it ...' he is saying, and as her thoughts wander she hears only odd words, 'the state of this bloody engine ... a tea towel ... and a dead sparrow ...'

Through the window you can see across the playing field to the motorway, which is pretty at this distance; nothing more than a string of lights and the distant drone of a man snoring in the next room. To the west lie the new estates, where all the streets are named after poets: Keats Avenue, Shelley Street, Coleridge Way. They pulled down rows of old terraces to make way for the estates, replacing them with culs-de-sac of four-square, orange-bricked houses like blocks of processed cheese. The summer they were built, all the local children would head up there in the evenings, clamber over the breeze-blocks, pull back the tarpaulins and peer into the cement mixers. That was the summer she really got to know Jimmy. A rowdy boy with brown arms, playing three-and-in against a half-built wall.

She looks across the table. He is jabbing fork-prongs into taut sausage skin, an angry spurt of pork fat falling on to the mashed potato. He doesn't look much different to all those summers ago. At twenty-three his face is still boyish, his jaw still set in concentration. Eating is to Jimmy a game of speed and strategy, the three-and-in of the dining table, and he does not so much clear his plate as sweep across territory. She watches him, knife and fork held in determined fists, shoulders rounded and head bowed, his body bending in close to the plate. She watches the dart of fork to mouth, the clamp of teeth against cutlery, the lick of the knife, the frantic chewing, jaw clicking, mashed potato slopping to and fro, lips making a light 'puh-puh-puh' as if smoking a pipe. She watches as he takes a slice of bread and mops his plate. She watches him lick his gravied fingers, push his plate away and belch. And she seethes, jaw tightening, teeth little millstones, grinding. 'Beg pardon,' he says, and sniffs. She wonders vaguely if it were ever acceptable to leave somebody because of their table manners.

Living with someone reveals a nest of habits: remote controls in the middle of the floor, teabags in the sink, toenail clippings in the carpet, sniffing, scratching, snoring. Quite inevitably one particular habit will become invested with such bilious hatred that it rises above all the rest: bigger, fatter, the queen of the colony. And for Jeannie, this has become Jimmy's eating habits.

Mornings were worst. Mornings meant cereal. Mornings meant the rapid clatter of spoon against bowl, the gulping of milk, the lifting of bowl to lips and then the long, final, excruciating slurp of the dregs. It was the same way he slurped soup and slurped tea. It was the same wet, airless way he kissed her. It was the reason she no longer let him go down on her in bed, because lying there, eyes studying the ceiling, she had the feeling of being nothing more than a bowl of Shredded Wheat.

Mostly it was the noise. She has never met anybody so singularly, unapologetically noisy as Jimmy. He walks loudly, talks loudly, closes doors with a slam. On the telephone he bellows. When he goes to the bathroom she braces herself for the sound of urine thundering triumphantly into the toilet bowl. In the street he spits volubly on to the pavement.

There had been a brief period at school when spitting was quite the thing, when all the boys and some of the tougher girls would spend their time hawking up phlegm and propelling it on to the playground. For at least two terms it was impossible to walk through the yard without encountering globules of spittle. In some small way, there was something pleasingly vernacular about the habit: the children's dredging up of chalk dust and tar and the mucus that accumulates in a wet climate reminiscent of the local miners, their fathers and grandfathers, clearing their lungs of coal dust each morning. Most of the boys had grown out of the spitting, the way the girls had given over such affectations as wrinkling down their school socks in perfect symmetrical pleats and back-combing their hair. But not Jimmy; he still sniffed and coughed and spluttered with gusto.

This is not to say that Jeannie is without her own unappealing habits. She cracks her knuckles and she picks her feet and her hair has a way of clinging on to the house, clustering in dusty corners, tumbleweeding across the hallway, and lingering on pillowcases and jackets. Jimmy would find it, great eely strands tangled around the plughole, and pull at it, like a well-rooted weed, gripping on to the very plumbing of the building.

'All right, Jeans?' Jimmy asks.

'What?' She looks up, startled. 'Sorry,' she mutters,

'I was miles away.' On her plate, her dinner sits half-cold.

'I was saying is there owt on the telly tonight?'

'I dunno ...' She prods the mashed potato. 'We should sort that seating plan though, else your mum'll be on at us again.'

'Yeah ...' Jimmy turns up the radio. 'Let's leave it till the weekend, eh?'

Planning a wedding, Jeannie has noticed, is a finicky and solitary task, much like needlework. Jimmy offers little practical assistance, and she is left alone to stitch together the elaborate pattern of families and friends. She lies awake at night trying to remember the names of all his cousins. Her own family is big enough, but his sprawls out across town, springing up from street to street like bindweed.

'Let's elope,' she said to Jimmy, once. 'Come on, let's just go to Gretna Green. There'll be no Auntie Gladys, no frouffy dresses, no first dance ...'

'I'm looking forward to the first dance,' he said, leaned back in his chair and folded his arms behind his head.

'You are not!' She sat down on his knee and cupped his face in her hands. 'Jimmy, you cannot dance for toffee. And we haven't even chosen a song yet. So I think, all in all, it would be best if we just went to Gretna.'

He laughed, wrapped his arms around her waist and kissed her forehead. 'It'll be fine, love,' he said. 'And besides, Gretna? My mam would never forgive us!'

Jimmy's mother is stewed with a sturdy practicality. She has a neat face and small hands and a stout little body generally encased in a bright blouse and ski pants. She smells of Windolene and oven chips. For the last month, barely an evening has gone by without her calling to discuss some detail or other related to the wedding. 'Jeannie love, I was thinking about the Scotch eggs …' she will begin. And as she talks, Jeannie can picture her, standing in the kitchen on the cordless telephone, before the cork pinboard with its calendar, parish newsletter, postcards from Tenerife. Jimmy is the first of her four sons to get married, and she is approaching the event with the same thoroughness she usually reserves for cleaning the bathroom.

Jimmy's father is ruddy-cheeked and always in a polo shirt, the hairs of his forearms frequently matted with paint. He breeds rabbits in a hutch in the back garden, and sometimes you will find him out there, smoking a cigarette and talking to them softly: 'Alreet, Snowy lass, it's a cowd'un t'neet, eh?'

In the early years of their courtship Jimmy and Jeannie would spend Friday nights with his parents, watching television; an endless run of game shows and chat shows and soap operas. They would sit, lodged in the sofa, eating toffees and drinking endless mugs of tea until his parents went to bed and they could fumble quietly in the dark. It had seemed so mature then, a thing to brag about at school, though as the video clock blinked in the darkness of the lounge, and his hand slid under her jumper, she always felt awash with a strange sadness, the feeling of being far from home and lost at sea.

They got engaged two years ago in Blackpool. It was the third Saturday in May, warm and bright, though a harsh wind scudded off the Atlantic. They booked into a cheap B&B, where there was no front gate, and the landlady answered the door in a blue satin dressing-gown, and where a large square of the bedroom carpet had been cut out and replaced with a piece of another carpet with an entirely different pattern. When they first arrived, Jeannie had opened the wardrobe doors and pulled out all the drawers. She found three moth-balls, a packet of Top Trumps and a Gideon Bible.

They went down to the Pleasure Beach, where it smelled of candy floss and chip-fat, and small children squalled and tantrumed in the queue for the dodgems. They went on the waltzers and shot plastic ducks. They walked along the front, and she studied every elderly couple they passed thinking: 'That'll be us one day.'

Away from the town, away from familiar surroundings, they found that they had little to talk about. They reminisced over childhood trips to the seaside; they laughed at tacky souvenirs and saucy postcards; they bought ice creams and sticks of Blackpool rock. But as they walked in silence along the pier, she felt a strange, sulphurous resentment towards him. She leaned against the railings and stared out at the vast grey sea, enjoying the violent cawing of the gulls, the waves that thundered against the pier, surf spat up into her face by the great gulps of wild, blustery air.

In the evening they'd got dressed up and gone for an Italian meal. She was so distracted by the fact her hold-up stockings kept falling down that she did not notice Jimmy nervously eating all of the breadsticks. She ordered gnocchi, though she had no idea what it was. Jimmy slurped his spaghetti, drank his wine too fast, shuffled his neck in his smart shirt. They had nothing to say to each other over dinner, either, so she listened to the couple at the next table bickering over bathroom suites. She couldn't stomach the gnocchi. Instead she mushed them neatly together and waited until the waitress took the plates away and she could order a bowl of Neapolitan ice cream. Three spoonfuls in, Jimmy said her name in such a way that she thought he might be ill. 'Are you all right?' she asked. 'Will you marry me?' he said quickly.

She looked down at the ice cream, vanilla and strawberry and chocolate blurring together in the bottom of the bowl. She looked at the speckles of grease on the tablecloth and the candlestick and the small bowl of parmesan and the plastic cheese plants and the waiter standing before the door that led to the street where two girls were rollerskating up and down the pavement, and she saw that she was trapped. She looked across at Jimmy, his face pale and anxious and terrible. 'Yes,' she said.

Back at the B&B she went to the bathroom along the hall. She washed her face and brushed her teeth and stared at herself in the mirror. She opened the bathroom window and breathed in the smell of chip paper carried on the cold wind. When she got back to the room Jimmy was asleep, and in the dark she rolled down her stockings and shuffled out of her dress and lay down on the unfamiliar sheets. She lay awake all night, staring at the hunched shape of the wardrobe, listening to footsteps on the stairwell, relieved when the morning came, and the light soaked through the thin curtains, and the air was filled with the sound of the gulls.

All the way home they planned the wedding. There was an excitement to her voice, but in the wing mirror her reflection stared back, hollow-eyed and grey. They would be married in the Catholic church, of course, and the reception would be at the Social Club, where their parents drank, and next Saturday they would head into town and choose a ring. Jimmy was quite giddy with it now, singing along to the radio and drumming his fingers on the steering wheel. At every set of traffic lights he leaned over and kissed her cheek.

They moved in together shortly after that; signed a lease on the house, crammed her belongings into the back of Jimmy's car and drove across town. Neither of them really knew what they were doing, and for those first few weeks the house carried an air of hesitation: they moved around each other awkwardly, lived off oven chips and baked beans, bought things they had previously only known their parents to buy: light bulbs, J cloths, bleach. Bin-bags of clothes sprawled on the bedroom floor; teacups went unwashed; they used a toaster left by the previous tenant that rattled with someone else's toast crumbs. Then slowly the house began to acquire a sense of permanence, they unpacked the bin-bags, cleaned the bath, placed an order with the milkman, and gradually their relationship fell into a routine, albeit one largely dictated by the television schedule, an itinerary of soap operas, sport and occasional sex.

The sex was not good. It was wordless and rushed, like a silent film car-chase. Afterwards he would always fall back on to the pillow with a breathless 'thanks love', as if what had just occurred was no more intimate than the making of a cup of tea. The first time they slept together Jeannie was fifteen, and so nervous she couldn't untie her shoelaces. She recalls the awkwardness, and the discomfort and how, too shy to mention contraceptives, she spent the days following repeatedly punching her stomach. But of the act itself she remembers strangely little, rather she recalls the greasy smell of his pillowcase and the view of pylons and garage roofs from under his curtain. She remembers the scent of his aftershave, and the nape of his neck grown clammy and soft. She recalls the sound of an old Smokey Robinson record, and then the clunk and scrawl as the music ended and the record made its slow, blank revolution beneath the needle. They had sex a lot back then, embraced it the way that teenagers embrace all vices: smoke till they wheeze, drink till they're sick. She would head to Jimmy's house after school and they would drink cups of tea then lie kissing on his bed, breath sweet and milky, tongues thick with tannin, fingers edging round waistbands.

These days when he tries to kiss her she pulls her head away, lets his lips meet her cheek, her neck, her shoulder, anywhere but her mouth. She has grown as impassive towards the act itself as waiting for the kettle to boil. 'Was that all right?' he will ask, occasionally, and she will nod, unable to speak, suddenly crying, struck dumb by the thought that this is it, for ever.

Eight o'clock, curtains still open, and the night sky an inky blue, the television showing a police drama: stern-faced officers drinking coffee back at the station, a lot of shouting and flipcharts and mackintoshes. Jimmy sits on the sofa, legs splayed, arms folded. She still loves his arms, strong and hairy and freckled, their undersides all pale and sinewy and soft, like turning over a leaf. She leans across and brushes her face against them. They smell of engines. He strokes her face, takes her hand

and absent-mindedly begins fiddling with the tips of her fingers, pressing the skin away from the nail-bed. 'I recognise that Sergeant Wilkinson,' he says. 'What else has he been in?'

She wishes he would shut up. She kisses the freckles, slides a hand under his T-shirt and up to the warmth of his chest. She keeps her eyes closed, trying very hard to rekindle the early desire she once felt for him. She lifts the hem of his T-shirt and kisses his belly. His skin tastes of soap and sweat. She kisses his ribs and his chest and his neck, runs her fingers down to his waist. 'Jeannie,' he sighs, 'I'm too tired, love. Let's just have a snuggle, eh?'

There are sirens on the television, blaring out across the lounge, loudly, intrusively. She pulls down his T-shirt and sits up straight. Jimmy puts his arm around her and they watch the television in silence. A man stands on a factory rooftop. Below him in the street stands a police officer with a loudhailer. A small crowd has gathered.

'I might put the kettle on,' Jeannie says.

'Oh grand,' Jimmy answers warmly. 'Have we got any of them Penguin biscuits left?'

In the kitchen, humiliation flares up her face, the sallow skin turned pink and blazing. She fills up the kettle and while it boils she begins the washing up, two days' worth, piled up on the counter. She starts with the glasses, then moves on to the bowls and the plates, working briskly, efficiently, until suddenly she stops, stands quite still with her hands in the bowl. The water rises halfway up her arms, grey and soapy and swimming with debris: a bloated cornflake, slicks of sausage fat. Down among the rubble of the cutlery she digs her nails into the remnants of yesterday's spaghetti. Her eyes blur and her lashes droop heavy and wet. From the living room comes the sound of the commercial break, jingles for Coco Pops and fizzy drinks, the sound of Jimmy laughing. The tears roll down her face, fall plumply into the dishwater. She digs her nails harder. Is this all there is? She wonders. Is this it?

CHAPTER THREE

The toilet seat was wet. She felt it press against the pale flesh of her thighs and she grimaced. Outside, the queue shuffled damply and sniffed, and from far below drifted the sound of buses sluicing through puddled streets. It was drizzling still. Beneath the cubicle door ran a line of tired shoes all spoiled by the rain: creased toes, sloped heels, cloudy white stains rising from their soles, as if giving up the ghost.

Amid the clatter and scrabble of the town, the Ladies' Powder Room had always articulated a quiet grandeur. It was there in the gilded armchairs, in the women resting their steady hips against the counter, bending in close to the glass to paint their faces. It was there in the faint nods they gave one another as they straightened their skirts, dabbed scent, pouted a little in the mirror. It was in the peach plumes of the tissue box. In the signs that read CAREFUL. VERY HOT WATER. In the door that swung open and brought with it the heavy smell of the cafeteria.

There were three cubicles, three hand basins, a hot air hand dryer, soap dispensers that, with some encouragement, blurted out a pink floral liquid, and a slim vending machine on the far wall containing sanitary towels and tampons. To the side extended a lounge area, with ruched curtains and a vase on the window ledge holding a spray of plastic roses.

It was in the next cubicle along that Jeannie once came to be sick after a Saturday afternoon spent drinking cheap strawberry wine in the park. When she rested her head against the cool porcelain basin and listened to the sound of the hand dryer ebbing and flowing she had felt soothed, somehow, by the sober dignity of the powder room. It was that same sense of decency that had eased the shame she once felt heading here to use a pregnancy test, a memory she has since condensed to the rustle of the chemist's bag with its scent of cotton wool and ointment, the warm rush of urine and the terror of waiting. When the line sprang up negative, she shoved it into the sanitary bin and headed out, propriety restored, to the escalators and the sunshine.

The Ladies' Powder Room is where she comes now to be alone. On her morning break, as today, she will lock herself inside and look through the dimpled windows at the pigeons shuffling on the ledge and the layers of droppings clinging to the stonework. In the warmer months, when the window stands ajar, there is a glimpse of pink feet, blue sky and soft grey feathers.

Today she is thinking of place settings. Of uncles and cousins and friends and acquaintances squashed around tables of eight, and claret napkins folded into fans. She is thinking of the seating plan written out on white card and placed on an easel by the door, of Jimmy's wish to name each table after a different make of car. She is thinking of the buffet, spread out on trestle tables beside the wall, of the platters of coronation chicken and sausage rolls. She is thinking of women's hands peeling back the clingfilm from the plates of ham sandwiches. Of trifle and cocktail sticks and roast beef. And she is thinking of how even the thought of it turns her stomach.

There are many things that concern Jeannie about her wedding. But the absence of any surge of happiness when she imagines the day itself causes her the most confusion. Should anyone happen to enquire about her feelings towards getting married she will of course heave a smile to her face, waggle her head up and down and say 'Oh yes, yes I can't wait!' They will duly ask about bridesmaid dresses and honeymoons and whether she is nervous. And maybe, she thinks, that is all it is. Nerves. She spreads her hands across her knees and looks at the blue-green veins. There are 30,000 million nerve cells in the body, a complex system of electrical impulses and bundles of nerve fibres, and together they are conspiring to make her doubt.

The staff toilets are different. You cannot think straight in there. They stand in a clotted yellow light, window-less and reeking of nicotine. There will always be someone leaning heavily against the sink with a cigarette, yawning and conducting a sulky conversation with some cubicled voice.

'And then he said he never even spoke to her and I said well why did Claire say she saw you then, eh? Think you can pull the wool over my eyes, do yer, yer fucken piece of shit?'

'I never liked 'im.'

'You and me mam.'

And the voice will exhale sharply, inflating the pause with cigarette smoke. From the cubicle there will come the sound of a toilet roll spinning and tearing, of the seat shifting, of zips and flushes and the door unlocking, and then the conversation will resume, shouted above the gush of the tap. 'And he's still got my fifty quid ...'

Finding quiet spaces in this town is difficult. For gener-ations its inhabitants have stood in rows: in terraced houses, in factory assembly lines and dole queues, in the mines, in the mills, in the queue for the bus and the bakery, and when all is all done and dusted, they have been laid out in neat earthy lines in the cemetery, to be strolled among on Sunday afternoons, in the same way they once were set out newborn and wailing in the rows of bassinets at the maternity ward. And so the days in this town seem little more than a procession, heavy feet falling one after another, a conveyer belt of lives.

Here, people live cheek by jowl, huddled close on doorsteps and in backyards, peering over fences and rooting out each other's business. People watch, people talk, and so one finds privacy where one can; quiet thoughts in public bathrooms; late-night couplings in the churchyard, with its dark elms and shadowed corners. Pale roaming hands at work on unlit benches; muffled unions made against rough stone, on damp grass, among the well-plotted roses.

When Jeannie and Jimmy were courting, they would bill and coo round the back of the sweet factory. They would drive up to a hill that looked out over the lights of this town and the next and the one after that. Sometimes they would head out to the coast, killing time in the arcades till it was nearly dark and you could drive up to the beach, ostensibly to catch the sunset. But you could never see the sea, just flat, dun sand stretching for ever. You would turn off the radio in case you flattened the battery, and then the only sound would be the press of lips and tongues, the creak of car seats, the faint click of a bra unclasped. And in the end you weren't alone, not really. You were just one more steamed-up car, in a row of other steamed-up cars.

After work this Thursday evening Jeannie heads up to the railway station, to the weary part of town where the Christian bookshop and the discount carpet store sit. When the railway came here in 1856 it arrived in a screech of dirt and grease and a terror of noise. The mayor was there in his gold chains, and a brass band played 'Rule Britannia'. The station now is a low, mild building remodelled in the 1970s, with glass doors that open and shut blankly, as a cow chews cud.

Inside it is quiet. A short queue stands before the ticket office window, and there comes a man's voice saying flatly: 'Blackburn. Return,' as his umbrella drips gently on to the asphalt floor. The foyer is a pale yellow, with walls that slide into a soft curve at the base, and hard metal benches with the raw glint of modernity. Jeannie glances up at the monitors, at the twitching list of departures and arrivals, then pushes through the heavy orange door into the Ladies.

Paper towels are strewn all across the floor, they concertina across the sinks and the baby-changing unit, their edges turning dark and damp. Daylight looks down cataracted by the skylight, and the air that rises to meet it is heavy with bleach and wet paper towels and urine.

The lock is broken and she keeps her hand on the cubicle door, pressing it shut. There is no seat and no toilet paper, and she fishes around in her pocket for a tissue. On the wall hangs a glob of bubblegum, hard-bitten indentations still visible, and next to it the words 'fuck you' and a sticker advertising a long-dead club night.

It has always seemed to Jeannie that there is something strangely comforting in the anonymity of public lavatories, from the cubicles of infant school, their toilet roll emblazoned with the words: NOW WASH YOUR HANDS, to the nightclub powder rooms and their surly attendant proffering paper towels, perfumes and lollipops. And while the railway toilets are not, owing to the stench and disorder, a place she would ever head to with the purpose of thinking, as the powder room at Pemberton's, it is nevertheless somewhere to which one can escape.

It has been a long day. A promotion on a new moisturiser, advertised gaily on the local radio station, has brought customers flocking to the counter. The moisturiser in question is a pale gloop smelling vaguely of apricots that comes in a white tub with a silver lid and the promise of a radiant, youthful complexion. Of course, few youths in this town have ever had a complexion one might consider radiant. From childhood onwards their faces bear the same grey sheen as their parents': a sallowness that no amount of scrubbing can remove and no cheap panstick concealer can ever truly hide.

But still they try. They cleanse and they tone, they exfoliate, they moisturise. They invest in brightening lotions and foundations and powders. They press shimmer to their cheekbones in an effort to catch the light. They fall for every cheap line like a plain lonely woman who longs for affection. Today's promotion encompasses not only the moisturiser but also an apricot-coloured washbag with a silver clasp, and inside samples of other St Emmanuelle products. The washbags arrived last week, swathed in clear plastic and with a set of selling instructions for the perfume girls to learn by rote. And so now, sitting on a seatless lavatory in the railway station, Jeannie's mouth feels clogged by the same jingle of words she has repeated faithfully all day; they stick to her teeth and fur her tongue: '… a visible difference in two weeks … and if you buy any other face product you get the washbag free!'

Half the reason she enjoys the squalor of the railway toilets is that they seem a world away from the perfection of the make-up counter, where everything is clean and bright and pastel-hued. It is an era in which cosmetic houses have grown enamoured with science and so the department store counters have acquired something of a clinical edge, with just enough frippery still to seem indulgent. Jeannie's uniform, therefore, hovers halfway between that of an air hostess and laboratory technician. She looks at the regulation American-tan tights, pushed down to her knees in wrinkles of fleshy nylon, and now she thinks not of the worries brought about by her wedding but of the sheer repulsiveness of tights, of double-stitched toes and reinforced gussets and of the sight of them wrinkled up on the floor by the bed like a used condom.

The mirror above the sink is not a real mirror but a long reflective strip bolted to the tiles which you cannot smash and which shows your face back, distorted and broken and dark. Someone has carved the name Shelley into its surface. Only the cold tap works, and the soap is a small yellow sliver, hard and latherless, and yet she performs the dance of washing as some kind of courtesy, holding her hands under the feeble breath of the electric hand dryer before wiping them on her skirt. Through the door struggles a woman laden with plastic bags and a toddler in a purple anorak. As Jeannie heads back outside she hears the woman's voice call out coarse and shrill like a gull: 'Pull your pants down, Jessica! Pull your pants down!'

Beneath the underpass, around the puddle that seeps across the concrete, and up the stairs to Platform 2, shoes smacking enjoyably against the damp steps. Rain drips from the verandah. The monitor shows a list of fluorescent green numbers and destinations: fifteen minutes

till the Crewe train. Wind whips along the platform spit-
tling rain, and the sky looks white and fierce. Jeannie
stands on the very edge. There are bleached-out chocolate wrappers strewn across the line, coins and bubblegum
and cigarette butts, fizzy pop cans rusting. Weeds scrawl
around the tracks.

Once the railway network around here bloomed.
From its heart at Manchester it spread out across the
region in a system of lines and stations, veins and ventri-
cles. But with the arrival of cars, the smaller stations
closed; the windows were boarded up, the lines became
overgrown with bindweed and Indian balsam, and dande-
lions forced their way up through the cracks in the plat-
forms. They were eerie places, haunted by the ghosts of
long-dead merriment: empty beer bottles, aerosols and
bags that perhaps had held glue. Still, on the Friday nights
of her teenage years they would head to one or other of
the old stations, away from the gaze of adults, to drink
cider, and spit.

The line here runs all the way down to London and
up to Glasgow. There are services to Liverpool, Preston,
Blackpool. Not far from here is another line that shunts
trains back and forth between Southport and Buxton,
through local stations like Gathurst, Hag Fold, Atherton,
Daisy Oak, slow dusty trains that rattle and hack their
way along the line so that it feels less that one has arrived
by the splendour of rail travel than been forcibly coughed

up at one's destination. Here at the bigger station the high-speed trains canter past, swift and sleek and brutal; you feel their approach against your legs first, rumbling up beneath your feet and the wind flickering against your calves.

A woman's voice crackles over the tannoy: 'The five thirty to Crewe has been delayed by ten minutes.' It is an automated announcement, glued together from pre-recorded tapes, and the words sit together at awkward angles, like people in a doctor's waiting room.

It is too cold to stay outside, and Jeannie is pleased to find that the station café is empty and warm. The boy behind the counter is wearing an old navy-blue hat that sits at odds with his regulation tabard, as a kind of mild protest. He is resting his head on his hands and staring down at a newspaper crossword puzzle, and when he looks up she sees his face is pale and open, like an O, and that he has newsprint smudged on his fingers. 'All right,' he says, and nods, stands up, rests a hand against the Formica. He is tall and skinny and there are bags beneath his eyes, but his mouth is alive and pursed like a beak.

'Cup of tea,' she says.

He nods again. 'Right you are,' he says, and reaches for a tower of polystyrene cups. 'You know the French don't drink their tea with milk.'

The hot-water urn huffs and snorts. Her gaze falls

loosely on the magazine rack: rows of puzzle books and women's weeklies full of weight-loss tips and real-life stories about bigamists and CB radio romances. 'The French eat horses,' she says, back at the counter and fishing out a fifty pence piece. He laughs. 'Yeah. What the fuck do they know, eh?'

Jeannie sits on one of the high chairs at the window. 'Here,' he says, 'have this if you want,' and he pushes a small plate carrying a Chelsea bun across the table. 'Well,' he adds quickly, 'it'll be stale tomorrow.' She stares at the bun. 'Thanks,' she says.

'I was there not long ago.'

'Where?'

'Paris.'

'That where you got your *chapeau*?'

He laughs and blushes a little. 'Nah, Manchester,' he says, slides into the seat next to her, and tears off a piece of the bun. 'Anyway, don't you know they all wear berets in France?'

'Oh yeah,' she says, pressing a piece of candied peel between her finger and thumb. 'And stripy jumpers, right?'

'Mmm-hmmm. Stripy jumpers, berets and they all have these big twirly moustaches. Even the women.'

'Bloody hell,' she struggles to keep her voice sombre, 'I had no idea.'

And there didn't seem much to say after that. They

stared out at the people waiting on the opposite platform: a portly man in a beige overcoat, and a little further
down a woman with neat white hair and a tartan bag at
her feet.

'Think they're on a date?' he wonders.

'Almost definitely,' she replies, and they lapse back
into silence.

'You been to Paris?' he asks eventually.

'Nah. We went to Calais once.'

'Who's we?'

'School. First year. Took the coach down to Dover
then the ferry and then to some supermarket and a café
and then back on the ferry. Forty twelve-year-olds all
puking up Nutella and *citron pressés* into the Channel.'

'Nice,' he says. 'You should go to Paris. You'd like it.
It's proper beautiful.'

'Yeah.' She fiddles with her teacup. 'Well anywhere's
got to be better than this place, eh?'

The tannoy bursts into life: 'The delayed five-thirty
train for Crewe is now approaching Platform 2.'

She gulps her tea. 'Ta,' she says, 'for the cake.'

'That your train is it?'

'Yeah.' She stands, and the crumbs tumble off her skirt.

'Where you going?'

'Nowhere.'

She is outside. The engine smell fills her nostrils and
she feels the warm rumble of the train against her face.

She starts at the far end of the platform and walks down the length of the train, catching glimpses of the world inside the carriages: the luggage stacked up and the tea trolley halfway along Coach D, all the faces, dim behind the glass, reading papers, caught in animated conversation, staring out at this drab, grey station. When she gets to the end of the platform she stands on the pale concrete promontory jutting out between the lines, where the wind jostles her hair and the rain spits in her eyes. She waits to hear the whistle, and when it comes it seems far away, like a shout in the night. The stationmaster waves his arms and the train pushes towards her, gathering speed, so that the final carriages rush by in a blur of grey. It feels something like shoving your head under water. When the train has gone, when the air is quiet again, she walks back along the platform. It is almost dark now. She looks up at the café window and sees the boy still sitting there, watching. She lifts her hand, and he winks at her through the glass.

It would be three weeks until she got to know his name and even then it did not come directly from him. The stationmaster popped his head around the door one day and called out, 'Eh, Danny-boy, make us a cup of tea, it's ruddy freezing out 'ere.'

Later he would tell her that he preferred it when people called him Daniel. 'But you know how it is round here,' he said with a jerk of the head, 'they call you by your surname or your nickname. Never your real name.'

She smirked a little at him. There was something so deliberate and dusty about the formality of Daniel. 'What was your nickname?' she asked and he blushed. 'Go on!' she said, and sipped her tea.

'Tufty,' he said eventually, and the tea came flying out of her mouth and her nose.

'TUFTY?'

'Cos of my hair,' he said, and lifted his cap to reveal a head of reddish-brown tufts. 'What's your name then?' he said, in an attempt to sober up the conversation.

'Jeannie,' she said.

'Can I call you Jeannette?' he asked.

'You most certainly cannot,' she said briskly. 'I hate that name. It was my auntie's. God only knows why they chose to saddle me with it too.'

She had gone to the station every Tuesday and Thursday evening since they first met, stopping first at the ladies, then for a cup of tea in the café, and then heading out to watch the Crewe train pass through. It was only after their fifth or sixth meeting that she noticed how she kept her left hand, with its neat little engagement ring, stationed firmly beneath the tabletop when she was talking to him. It was March now, and her wedding seemed to drift towards her, big and white, like an iceberg approaching a cruise ship, and she viewed it with a mixture of bafflement and dread. Perhaps more than anything, she enjoyed talking to someone who knew nothing about it, who spoke to her about subjects that had nothing to do with weddings.

She learned that he was from Macclesfield, that he lived with his grandad in town, that when he talked he had a way of crinkling his mouth that implied a state of perpetual amusement. And she found that in the hours she spent at Pemberton's restocking the eye make-up remover and straightening the lipsticks, it pleased her to think of him standing behind the little counter at the railway station, making cups of tea and hot chocolate, and carefully placing Danish pastries on small white plates.

One afternoon, on his break, he walked down to Pemberton's and watched her, moving gently behind the counter. She was talking to a large woman in a plum-coloured raincoat, dabbing something on the back of her hand and nodding slowly. The perfume hall shocked him, the strange swell of scents, all the sharp, orange women. 'Can I help you?' asked one. Her accent was broad and her breath smelled of menthol cigarettes. He felt dazed and nauseous. He looked at Jeannie and saw how ludicrously out of place she was, with her sweet drab hair and her long pale hands.

'What is it about the Crewe train?' he asked that evening when she came into the café. It had unsettled him slightly to see her out of context, to realise that she had another life beyond the station.

She shrugged. 'I dunno. London seems too far, Preston seems too close.'

He looked at his hands; today the fingers were stained with drinking chocolate. 'For what?'

She looked at his hands too, at the raggedy nails and the whorls of his fingers. 'I dunno,' she said again.

But she did know. London seemed too far to run away to. There were days when it seemed that boarding a train and running away was the most logical answer to avoiding marrying a man she wasn't sure she loved. She would get on a train and sit in a forward-facing seat, with a table. After a little while, after they were past Warrington Bank Quay, perhaps, she would stand up and walk along the carriage to the buffet car and buy herself a cup of tea, or perhaps something a little stronger to still her jangling nerves. And then she would head back through the carriages, with her paper buffet bag in one hand and the other steadying herself against the seats as she passed, and she would pause as she stepped through the gap between the carriages, where the ground jostled and shook, and you saw how feebly one carriage was connected to the next, and it made you feel a little alive, somehow, as if your life hung by a thread.

CHAPTER FOUR

On Saturday nights the town springs alive; bodies swarm up through the streets as salmon swim upstream to spawn. They wear tight, white dresses, bare legs and no coats. They wear short-sleeved shirts and strong aftershave. They fold their arms across their bodies to hoick up their bosoms and huddle themselves warm. At the crossroads in the centre of town they congregate, circling the bars, cawing like gulls, standing in line before the nightclub bouncers. Their legs are mottled pink and blue.

All Saturday afternoon the perfume hall is busy, its aisles full of women choosing paints and powders for the evening ahead. At Jeannie's counter sits a display of the new St Emmanuelle fragrance Blue Hyacinths. It is heavy and wet and floral, a synthetic impersonation of the spring flower, and reminds her of the old-fashioned scents her grandmother likes to wear.

'This is nice,' says Michaela, picking up the blue glass bottle and sniffing it lightly. 'Bit old lady though.' Michaela works on the Cordalie counter across the opposite side of the hall. She is small and buxom and brown, and her lipstick is a startling shade of tangerine. This is only the third time she has spoken to Jeannie. However, the arrival of a new perfume girl, a pale, doughy young woman named Julie, whom the other girls dislike even more, has allowed Jeannie to shuffle up the pecking order.

'Are you coming for a drink with us tonight?' Michaela asks, finger now knuckle-deep in a jar of anti-wrinkle cream.

'Yeah, all right,' Jeannie answers with some hesitation. She notices that Michaela has foundation stuck in her hairline. 'Where are you going?'

'Round town.' Michaela is spritzing her neck with Blue Hyacinths. 'Gonna find us some fellas!' she winks, and trots back to her counter.

The air is thick with hairspray, rising up to the ceiling in great midgey clouds. Jeannie stands by the hand dryer in her jeans and trainers and a pink blouse. She is gripping a blue plastic bag that holds her uniform, and she twirls its handles round and round her fingers. Even above the scent of the Elnett, she can smell the hyacinth perfume on her hair and her skin, taste it still on her lips.

The girls are getting dolled up. Kimberley is curling her eyelashes, April is dusting bronzer over her cleavage, Michaela is lining her lips with postbox-red pencil. 'Pass us that bottle, will ya?' she says, and smacks her lips together. Kimberley passes the bottle of cheap cherry brandy, and Michaela takes a long swig. 'Here, Jeannie,' she says and sticks out her hand. Jeannie takes the bottle and eyes it warily. The top is smeared with red lipstick. 'Tastes like shit,' says Michaela, 'but it'll keep you warm. Fucken winter.'

They wear tight-fitting dresses and high heels. 'Can you see me thong in this?' Nicola is standing on the toilet seat, looking backwards over her shoulder and squinting at the mirror.

Kimberley turns around briefly. 'Yeah,' she says matter-of-factly, and returns to her eye make-up.

Nicola reaches up under her dress, tugs down her knickers and shoves them into her handbag. 'Remind me to keep me legs closed,' she says.

'I remind you of that every week, Nicola,' smirks Michaela, 'but you never listen.'

They laugh, and even Jeannie smiles a little. She likes the way the brandy has numbed her lips and made her teeth taste sweet.

'What were his name last week, Nic?' asks April.

'Barry, or Gary, or something,' Nicola says with a shrug. 'I were mad in love with him till Tuesday, but he never called me. Hey, Jeannie, how long you been with your fella?'

'Six years,' says Jeannie.

'Six blinkin' years!' Nicola gasps. 'I've never been with a fella longer than six weeks, me!'

'Six days, more like,' mutters April. 'Want me to do your eyes for ya, Jeannie?' she asks, and beckons her over to the sinks, where she has a small compact of eyeshadows and blushers and lipsticks. She takes the little brush and sweeps silver glitter gently across Jeannie's eyelids, then adds several strokes of mascara. Jeannie blinks. In the mirror her eyes stare back prettily. 'Thanks,' she smiles.

'Well,' says April, 'you have to make an effort on a Saturday night, don't you? C'mon, ladies,' she calls to the others, 'let's get fucken trolleyed!'

Up the steps of Harry's Bar, the carpet runs a worn maroon, and you can still see the stains where revellers have been sick on evenings gone by. Upstairs the room churns with cigarette smoke and the tinny beat of chart hits. People are dancing and shouting and flirting, half-drunk and lairy. Behind the bar a blond man is making cocktails in a blender, and above him a blackboard reads: Fluffy Duck, Pink Flamingo, Blue Paradise.

'What you having?' Michaela nudges her in the ribs. 'I'm buying.'

'Oh, the pink one,' says Jeannie. 'Thanks.' It looks just like strawberry milkshake, frothy and pale and served with a striped straw.

'Cheers, ladies!' shouts Nicola. 'Get 'em down yer!' The drink tastes vaguely of fruit and strongly of alcohol.

'Christ. What's in this?' Jeannie coughs.

'Fucked if I know,' Nicola laughs. 'Puts hairs on your chest though, eh?'

A man in a green checked shirt approaches their table. 'Ey-up, ladies!' he says. His face is shiny and his hair lacquered into spikes. 'You're all looking beautiful tonight, if I may say so!'

'Darren, have you met Jeannie?' April says, with a roll of the eyes.

'Delighted to make your acquaintance,' he replies and holds out a small, smooth hand, still clammy from his pint glass. His manner is polished, but his accent is scuffed and broad. 'And how do you know these fragrant ladies?' he asks with a nod to the others, and sliding into an empty seat.

'Jeannie's one of us, she works at Pemberton's,' Michaela says brusquely, stubbing out a cigarette. 'And she's engaged, so don't go getting any bright ideas, Darren.'

'Michaela, my dear, you know I only have eyes for

you,' he says, and under the table his hand slides up Jeannie's thigh. She pulls her leg away.

'You're so full o' shit, you,' says Michaela. There is, Jeannie senses, some history between Michaela and Darren.

'Michaela darling, that's not what you were saying last Saturday night,' he smiles, and his hand strays back to Jeannie's knee.

'I were drunk!' Michaela snaps.

'Yeah, and I think I like you better that way,' Darren laughs. He leans in close to Jeannie, so close she can feel his breath warm on her neck: 'She might be a mardy cow now,' he stage whispers, 'but a couple of shandies and then she's all sweetness and roses.' Beneath the scent of his breath and the aftershave and the hair lacquer, Jeannie can smell the sourness of sweat and cigarette smoke, clothes left too long in the machine and other women's perfume pressed into his shirt by Saturday night embraces.

'Hey, Jeannie, want another?' Kimberley is leaning over the table. You can see down her cleavage to the folds of her belly.

'No, ta, I'd best be off. Jimmy'll be waiting and that.'

'Go on!' Darren stretches his arm around her shoulders, and she feels his fingers pressing damply through the sleeve of her blouse. 'It's Saturday night!' He shouts towards the bar: 'Get her another Kim!' His arm stays where it is, though his fingers slip to her side, find the underwire of her bra.

'Fucking hell! Have you seen the arse on that new barman?' says Kimberley, returning with a tray of Fluffy Ducks and a packet of cigarettes.

'That lad?!' Michaela turns and gawps. 'He's hardly legal love! Do you want to get arrested?'

'I'm not saying I want to do owt with him!' Kimberley laughs. 'I'm just … admiring at a distance, is all.'

The Fluffy Duck tastes much the same as the Pink Flamingo. She swishes it about in her mouth as Darren's hand slides slowly down her back, finds its way under the hem of her blouse to the cold, pale skin below. It doesn't feel altogether unpleasant. She takes another sip, his fingers pull at the waistband of her jeans. Maybe, she thinks, she should try a Blue Paradise next.

'What you up to tomorrow then Jeannie?' April leans across the table. Half her lipstick has relocated from her mouth to her straw.

Jeannie blinks, shuffles away from Darren's hand. 'Oh,' she says quickly, 'wedding stuff. We've got to choose all the food, you know?' Jolted by a sudden flash of guilt she downs the rest of her cocktail and slides out of her seat, a little shaky now as she stands. 'Have a good night,' she tells them.

'Oh, you off?' says Michaela. 'See you Monday! And don't do anything I wouldn't do!'

She runs quickly down the stairs, the carpet sticking to her feet and the feeling of Darren's fingers still warm against the small of her back.

Jimmy is in the Lion, three pints down. 'Hey hey!' he jeers as Jeannie pushes her way through the busy bar to his regular table. 'Here comes the bride!' She forces a smile and nods to Jimmy's friends, all piled around the table. There are pint glasses, crisp packets and cigarette butts. 'What have I missed?' she asks.

'Nothing, love, we've just been discussing our game plan for the match tomorrow.' He taps his right temple. 'Tactics!' he says, and grins.

'Jimmy,' she says with flat-voiced annoyance, 'we have to go to the Club tomorrow. We're meeting the caterers. You know that.'

'Jeans,' he kisses her on the cheek and she can smell the lager on him, 'we don't both have to be there, do we? It's a big match, this. And I won't know what I'm talking about anyway. I've told you before, I am a man who has never knowingly eaten a vol-au-vent.'

'That's not the point, Jimmy, I'm tired of doing all this wedding crap by myself.'

'Ooooooooh!' his mates chorus. They are burly young men, good-natured yet buckish, and tonight their faces are flamed with the joys of cheap ale and the weekend to come.

'C'mon, Jeans,' Jimmy says gently. 'This is womanly stuff, this. What do I know about cakes and flowers and all that pretty-girly shit?'

She glares at him fiercely, his face turned mushy with beer. 'I'll see you later,' she says, voice now chilly, then pulls on her coat and heads to the door. As she jostles her way out to the street she can hear him calling after her: 'Jeans! Jeannie!'

Striding up through the bus station, arms folded, bolstered by cherry brandy and cocktails, she passes lines of men sitting under the strip-lighting, early evening drinkers now waiting for buses back home to Hindley, Platt Bridge, Atherton. They are bundled up in winter coats, sipping cans of ale, reading the *Evening Post*, holding the same conversations they hold every Friday night, about the weather, the weekend, the wife. She is sick of the staleness of this town, the drudging routine of Saturday nights at the same pub, Sunday morning hangovers, afternoon football, evening roast, bed at ten, up at seven, breakfast, uniform, bus to work, the deadening sameness of it all.

She has reached the railway station. Outside, the minicabs sit in a long line, waiting for passengers from the Manchester train. At this hour on a Saturday night a low thrum of expectation hovers above the town, everyone is waiting, waiting for buses and trains and taxis, for drunkenness and dance floors and long, bleary kisses on the cab ride home. It is quiet inside the station. She thuds up the steps to Platform 1 and settles on the wooden bench, watching the Blackpool train, sitting in the station, engine humming. She wishes she could go back there, back to the B&B and the promenade and the Italian restaurant. She wishes she could take it all back. The waiting train has turned the air warm and faintly sweet with engine dust. She watches its dirty windows, its empty seats, fiddles with the small diamond ring on her left hand, slides it up over the knuckle, the nail, folds it into the palm of her hand.

'Hello, stranger,' Danny says, and slumps on to the bench beside her.

'Oh,' she says. 'Hi.'

She cannot look at him. Instead she stares blurrily at the train, doors open, lights on, empty, presses the diamond ring harder into the flesh of her palm.

'And what brings you here this evening?' he asks. 'Shouldn't you be off having a riot with your mates?' She shrugs and sort of gulps and he can see now that she has been crying. Mascara and silver glitter lie in dark trickles down her face. 'Hey,' he says, 'hey, it's all right, petal,' and rubs the smudges on her cheeks. 'What's happened?'

'Nothing,' she says, and smiles in a watery way. 'I was just thinking I'd love to go to the seaside.'

He laughs. 'Well I tell you what, Lady Jeannie, we'll do the next best thing.'

'What's that?'

'Come with me,' he says, and proffers an arm. She looks up at him, smiling under the platform lights, and cautiously loops her arm into his. They stroll together down the steps, beneath the underpass and out through the automatic doors.

'So why aren't you out having fun?' she asks out on the street, and delicately disengages her arm, anxious that someone might see her, parading through town with a strange man.

'Well,' he says, 'I don't know that many people round here. Only the bloke that runs the second-hand shop on Swinley Street, and the bald librarian, and the woman in the corner shop near ours. Oh, and my grandad and his mates – but they're a terrible lot; every Saturday night they get tanked up on mild and then go cruising for chicks.'

She laughs. 'There we are!' he says triumphantly. 'There we are! A laugh! An actual laugh. You had me worried there for a minute. I thought maybe we'd never hear you laugh again.'

She shakes her head. 'So how come you don't have any friends then? I mean apart from the librarian and that.'

'There's nothing wrong with me,' he insists. 'Honestly. I mean I had a lot of friends back in Macclesfield. But sometimes you just want a bit of peace and quiet, you know? None of that fussing, and everybody knowing your business.' He falls quiet for a moment. 'So what's at the seaside?' he asks.

'I just haven't been there for a bit,' she answers vaguely, and they each know they are hiding something.

They reach the path down to the canal. 'Now,' he says, jovially. 'I can't promise you a promenade or a pier, but I can offer you a towpath and the pleasure of my company. And this,' he says, taking a bottle of rum out of his jacket pocket.

'Is that all?' Jeannie laughs.

'Hang on,' he says, and pats his pockets. 'Hang on … Oh, yes, and these …' He brings out four toffees, two bus tickets and fifty-six pence.

She takes a toffee. 'OK then,' she says.

It is dark down on the towpath, and in the darkness she slides her engagement ring back on to its finger. A lamp on the bridge spills out a small milky pool of light, beyond which is blackness.

'Fuck,' she giggles. 'I can't see a bloody thing!' And then: 'What if we fall in?'

'We won't fall in,' he assures her. 'Let your eyes settle.'

They stand in silence for a few moments, listening to the soft lap of the water and the cars swishing by on the bridge. 'Oh!' she cries with sudden delight. 'There! I can see the path!'

'Good,' he says. 'And now that you've got your night

eyes, have a swig of this.' He hands her the bottle. 'It'll settle your nerves.'

'What nerves?' she asks, as she unscrews the top and a shock of strong rum hits her lips. 'I'm not afraid of anything.'

'Not even of sea snakes and pirates and the ghosts of bargemen past?' he says with mock incredulity.

'Not even them,' she says.

'Well then, you are going to make a fine travelling companion,' he tells her. Through the darkness she hears the slosh of rum, and then, as he raises it to his mouth, a sudden glint of lamplight strikes the bottle.

'Now, Jeannie,' he says, as they set off along the towpath, the earth chawing slightly underfoot. 'Are you familiar with wakes week?'

'The what?' she says.

'Turrible,' he says. 'Turrible, the youth of today. Wakes,' he tells her, 'were religious festivals, feasts of dedication to the parish church, when people stopped up all night, revelling. Now, when the factories came, wakes weeks were what happened all round here, when they shut up the mills, and everyone headed off to the seaside on the railways.'

'They did?' she asks.

'They did,' he assures her.

'Are you having me on?' She eyes him suspiciously through the dark.

'No. Now, each town had a different week. Round here it was the start of August. Back in Macclesfield we had Barnaby Week, for St Barnabas, in June.'

'How do you know all this?' she asks.

'Library. It pays to be in with the staff. Anyway, I reckon what we should do this evening is make this our own little wakes week.'

'I like it,' she said. 'Though I didn't bring my bathing costume.'

He laughs. 'Well to be honest, I'm not sure I'd advise swimming in the canal. You'd probably get Weil's disease. Or attacked by ducks.'

'How do you remember all this stuff?' she asks.

'I dunno, it just sticks in my head,' he says, and she can hear him unscrewing the rum. 'I like learning things.'

'Yeah. You know, I think you are the most knowledge-able person I've ever met,' she tells him.

'Thank you,' he says proudly, and hands her the bottle.

'So why the fuck are you working in a station buffet?' she demands.

'Well,' he clears his throat, 'it's just for the time being. Just till I work out my plan for world domination.'

'And how's that coming along?'

'Oh, you know,' he says, and his voice is droll, 'I've got as far as 'Invade Poland', and after that I'm at a bit of a loss.'

'Did you go to university?' she asks, and takes another sip of rum.

'Nah,' he says. 'I dicked about too much. Fucked up my exams.'

For a few minutes they say nothing. Across the other side of the canal stands one of the modern estates. Lights are on in some of the houses, and music floats across the water: a piano, and a man's voice brushing heavily against the night. It feels somehow intrusive, as if they are being spied upon, and it comes as a relief to reach the pitch darkness of the next bridge. 'Wait,' she says as they pass under. 'Feel this.' And she guides his hand to the rope-grooves in the stonework. 'I used to love touching that when I was a kid,' she says. 'It gave me the shivers.'

'Yeah,' he says quietly. 'Have you ever been to Hard-castle Crags? I used to feel the same up there. There's an old cotton mill, and a pond, and a hundred years ago it must've been all noise and industry. It's the way it's so quiet now, and the pond is so still.'

They walk on. 'How old are you?' she asks when they are well clear of the houses.

'Twenty-four,' he says. She hears a flick and a fizzle as he lights a roll-up, the flame splaying light on to his face. 'You?'

'Twenty-one.'

'And why the fuck are you working as a perfume girl?'

His face is gone again now, lost in the blackness. She

watches the glow of the cigarette dancing about in the dark.

'I haven't a fucking clue,' she says, and fights a sudden urge to cry. 'I left college, and I needed a job, and you know ...' She shrugs. 'It's just for the time being. Just till Poland, y'know ...'

'You're too good for it.'

'Thanks,' she says briskly. 'Actually, I'm really bad at it. I'm the worst perfume girl in the whole of Pemberton's, probably in the whole world, in fact.' And then, embarrassed, she changes the subject. 'Tell me some more stuff,' she says, and gives a short laugh. 'Educate me, library-boy.'

'What kind of stuff?' He draws heavily on the cigarette.

'Well,' she says, 'tell me about the canal.'

'The canal, the canal,' he says. 'Let's see, well, there are ninety-one locks the length of this canal, and your little town – our little town – runs twenty-one locks of it.'

'Blimey,' she says. 'Twenty-one locks.'

'Yep. A lock for every year of your life,' he tells her. 'Now, the canal is a haven for wildlife. Sticklebacks, for instance. The interesting thing about the stickleback is that it has no scales, and it is related to the seahorse. And what else? Water boatmen, of course, so called because their back legs are shaped like oars ... Are you still awake?'

'Yes,' she laughs, 'carry on, I'm listening.'

'Good,' he says, 'because I forgot to mention that there will be a test at the end of this. So the water boatman is, as I am sure you know, closely related to the back-swimmer, and the way to tell them apart is that the back-swimmer swims upside down. Got that?'

'Yes.' She can barely speak for laughing. 'Upside down.'

'Now, what else can we expect to see in the canal? Moorhens, of course, and coots, and the occasional king-fisher, and frogspawn soon, I should expect. What other stuff would you like to know?' he offers, enjoying his scholarly role and her apparent amusement.

'How come you really left Macclesfield?' she asks, now emboldened by rum. She sees the cigarette tip flare, then fall, blacked out suddenly underfoot.

'I got a girl pregnant.' He says it quickly, loudly, so boldly she knows he is ashamed.

'You did a runner?' she asks, stunned.

'No, no, of course not.' His footsteps stop. He touches her arm 'It wasn't like that.'

'What was it like?' she says softly.

'It was just a mess.'

'Did she ... Did she have it?'

'No. No she didn't,' he says blankly, and begins walking again. 'I was too young. We both were. I s'pose you'd call her my childhood sweetheart – a really lovely girl, you know? She's with someone else now. Happy.'

'Are you?' she asks.

'Right now, tonight, yes I am,' he tells her. 'I'm very happy.' They take another swig of rum. 'Let's have a toffee,' he says, and in the darkness the cellophane crackles. 'And what about you?' he says, voice muddied with caramel. 'Who's in Blackpool?'

'No one,' she says, and in the darkness she fiddles with her engagement ring. 'No one's in Blackpool.' She curls her toes with guilt, digs her fingernails into her palms.

The moon lies flat, now, on the canal, and away from the centre of town the dank smell of the water has given way to a sweetness, the scent of spring coming in. It is there, too, in the wet trees, and in the coots and the ducks rustling in the banks, and in the green rushes that, he tells her, will have grown taller than both of them come the summer. At some points, though, the mood of the canal will change, turn suddenly cold and dark. Then the water sits cheerless and spumey, clogged with feathers and sticks, drowned plastic bags and beer cans, bobbing.

They walk until it is light, and the sky is charged with birdsong; till the scent of sun-soaked blackthorn rises up sweet and soapy, and they can see the towpath beneath their feet running sandy and smooth. They walk far out from the town, out to where the air smells of milk and manure, and bullocks flood up to the fence, huffing damp breath. They look through the hedges and see way across the fields, past where the hogweed will grow, thick-stemmed and broad-flowered, in the summer months. Through the damp silence of early morning the hills seem mottled with age; speckled with sheep and cattle, veined with roads that glisten silver-blue under a sudden burst of sunlight. All along the footpath the ferns bow and curl their forelocks, and in amongst the budding branches sit the nooks where soon the courting chaffinches will build their nests.

And as they walk they talk, about the town and about the streets where they grew up, about the families and their friends, and the men that fish the canal banks with maggots under their tongues. They drink rum and they chew grass, and they take turns peeing behind the hedge. 'Don't look!' she laughs, crouching below the verge.

'I'm not!' he calls.

'Well then, what are you doing?' she shouts.

'Pissing!' he yells back.

It is fully light when they emerge from the towpath, up on to the bridge not far from her house. 'Did you enjoy your wakes week?' he asks, and his voice is hoarse and thin.

She nods. 'But we never sent any postcards,' she says sleepily.

He smiles. His eyes are half-closed, like a lizard's. 'Give us a hug,' he says. He grips her tightly, her face pressed up against the damp wool of his jacket, and he rests his head on hers. They stand like that for a long while, until a car rolls by and they part and turn their separate ways.

She does not look back. All the way home the streets are empty and still, and her footsteps echo along the rows of sleeping houses. At the far end of Atherton Road she can see the sunlight rising up over the trees. She feels glorious.

The milk is on the step and the door is on the latch. She leaves her shoes in the hall and creeps up the stairs, legs heavy, head thick, undresses quietly outside the bedroom door, leaves her clothes heaped on the landing, and slips into bed. Cold sheets against cold toes. Beneath the eiderdown she can feel the warmth of Jimmy, the air close to him stewed in beer and sweat and cigarettes. The light is slinking through the curtains, a glimpse of dusty windowpane. She scrunches her eyes and imagines herself a fly, a fat bluebottle, bashing again and again, over and over against the glass.

Chapter Five

On the bathroom ceiling, a pale fungus is flowering: smooth, soapy petals the colour of wet sand. Jeannie stands in her nightdress, looking up, trying to remember if it was there yesterday, and what should be done about it. She opens the window a few inches, as far as it will allow, and returns to her vantage point on the bathmat. From here she can see, now, the black mould shingling the paintwork.

The bathroom is a small, badly ventilated room, prone to damp, that sits at the top of the stairs. As with most of the terraced houses in the town, it was installed with much fanfare in the 1950s. Half the back bedroom was donated to the cause, a thin plasterboard wall hastily erected and papered over with a design of tea roses and swallows.

It is an awkward room, squeezed in like an extra guest at the dinner table, with a stark white suite and a window that offers a frosted view of the backyard and the spot where the outside toilet once stood. There is a heavy smell of wet air, of apple shampoo and damp towels; the carpet feels clammy underfoot and the toilet paper is cold and limp. Jeannie wraps a few sheets of tissue around her forefinger and prods the fungus; it does not move.

She has taken the day off for a wedding dress fitting in town. Her mother will be there, along with her sister, Dannielle, and her best friend, Marie. It will be, her mother announced the previous evening, 'a proper girls' day out'. Jeannie had grimaced down the telephone, and tried to mentally assemble an appropriate itinerary, cobbled together from romantic Hollywood films and the pages of women's magazines.

This morning, accordingly, she slept late, then painted her toenails and drank sweet tea with one eye on the cartoons. She lay in the bath and listened to the local radio station playing Sonny & Cher and Don McLean and adverts for caravans and bicycle shops. After a while the water grew cool, and she grew bored, and so she climbed out and dried herself and her nail varnish came off on the towel. She made various attempts to swaddle her hair glamorously in the hand towel, but in the end she dragged it up into a wet topknot. Now she opens the sample of marine mineral face mask she took from work, plasters its pale-green contents thickly across her face, and sits on the bathroom floor, against the radiator, reading a copy of *Woman's Own*.

There is something industrial about the private beauty routines of women: the shaving of legs and the bleaching of moustaches, the creams, powders, oils, the painting of faces, the eyelash curlers, girdles, stockings, the setting lotions, the rollers, clips, pins and tweezers. They are intricate machines, with pistons and pulleys, reels and rotors, performing the same intimate tasks over and over with a fine-milled precision.

Jeannie is reading a story about a woman who found love through CB radio, when the doorbell rings. Through the dimpled glass of the front door she can make out the familiar shape of her mother. She undoes the latch.

'Hi,' she says, and the face mask cracks around her mouth.

'Jeannie,' her mother says with exasperation, 'why aren't you dressed?'

They are due at the wedding dress shop at eleven o'clock. Jeannie looks blankly at her mother, distracted by the Barr's drinks lorry rolling by over her shoulder, thoughts of warm lemonade and cream soda. 'What time is it?' she asks, and flakes of face mask float on to the hall carpet. 'Quarter past ten,' her mother says. 'We'll be late if you don't get a move on. What on earth have you been doing all morning?'

Jeannie's mother is a solid woman, sturdier than her daughter, her body has been broadened by childbirth and biscuits, and she wields a somewhat practical demeanour; she wears her hair short for the sake of convenience and long ago succumbed to the charms of elasticated waistbands. As her daughter thunders up the stairs, she sways through to the kitchen and, out of habit, fills the kettle. And while her mother slips off her coat and finds the custard creams, Jeannie scrubs at her face, half-dries her hair, flings open her wardrobe door. She pulls on thick tights, a long black skirt and an old flannel shirt.

'Is that what you're wearing?' Her mother stands in the doorway holding two cups of tea.

Jeannie nods. 'Is it not OK?' She sees now that her mother has put on slightly more make-up than usual and is wearing gold earrings shaped like shells.

'Come on, love,' her mother says, edging the tea on to the bedside table, 'let's make a bit of an effort. It's a special day. What have you got in here?' She roots through her daughter's wardrobe. 'Here!' she says, triumphantly holding up a long pink floral dress Jeannie has not worn for years. 'I always liked you in this!'

The car is cold and smells of stale cigarettes. Her mother drives nervously, hunched over the steering wheel and too close to the kerb, while the radio plays an old Everley

Brothers song. Dannielle sits in the back seat, flicking through a magazine. She is seventeen and works in a hairdressing salon on the outskirts of town, shampooing and conditioning and sweeping up hair. There are few similarities that would suggest she and Jeannie are sisters; Dannielle is a cheerful girl with permed blonde hair, a sunbed tan and a steady stream of boyfriends.

'Has Jimmy got his suit yet?' her mother asks, casting her eyes towards the passenger seat and swerving toward the centre of the road as she does so.

'He's hiring one, Mum,' Jeannie sighs. They have had this conversation at least twice already in recent weeks.

'Hiring one?' Her mother shakes her head. 'Why doesn't he buy one? He'll need a suit again.'

'Mum, what does he want a suit for? He's a mechanic.' Jeannie watches a thin woman hurrying up the street, purse in her hand and carpet slippers on her feet. Her breath puffs out in cold white clouds before her, so that she resembles a small steam engine chugging along the pavement.

'You can't get married in a hired suit,' her mother is saying. 'Foster's Menswear has a sale on, I saw a sign in the window the other day ...'

'Hey, Jeannie,' Dannielle throws her magazine down, 'guess who's pregnant?'

Jeannie sifts through the names of Dannielle's friends and acquaintances. 'Who?' she says eventually.

'Lisa!' Dannielle gasps and widens her eyes for emphasis.

'Which Lisa?' It had always seemed that at least half of Dannielle's friends were called Lisa. It was a popular name in the year of her birth, and their father often remarked that there were seven Lisas born on the maternity ward that weekend alone.

'Little Lisa! You know!' Dannielle has a habit of speaking in exclamations. 'Big calves. Black hair. Lives by the curry house.'

Jeannie alights on a hard-faced girl who always smelled of hairspray. 'Oh. That Lisa. Who's the dad?'

'Some guy she shagged round the back of Maximes.' The dark alleyway that ran behind one of the town's nightclubs was a well-known destination for casual sex, and even when one walked along it in daylight it carried something of a post-coital air. 'She said he was from Manchester.' The swagger of the big city at least brings a gleam of sophistication to Lisa's situation.

They're made mothers early in this town. Firm, ripe youth stewed into maternal tenderness, hips spread, skin stretched, thighs thickened, their new selves accommodated by tracksuit pants, council flats and toddler groups. There were five pregnancies in Jeannie's final school year. It was thrilling at the time, a distraction from GCSEs and coursework and netball practice. But she hardly sees those girls these days. She heard Bernadette had another baby, and she saw Michelle in the Co-op once, her little boy three years old, tearing bags of cheese and onion crisps off the shelves.

Cranks' Wedding Dresses is a short walk from Pemberton's, lodged between a bakery and a shop selling model soldiers. There are three mannequins in the window, arranged against purple-swagged drapery: a groom in top hat and tails, a small bridesmaid in hooped peach satin, and a bride in an extravagant white ensemble, all tumbling lace, pleats and puffed sleeves, carrying a dusty bouquet of red roses and gypsophila. She wears a long veil and a tiara and a demure pink blush has been painted on to her plaster cheeks.

Marie is sitting on the window ledge eating a bacon barm. 'Hiya!' she calls brightly, and waves her greasy fingers. There is flour on her chin. Jeannie and Marie grew up three streets apart, they went to school together, sat next to one another in class, and when Marie got married last summer, Jeannie was her bridesmaid. She is tall and bony with curly brown hair, and she works in the musical instrument shop on King Street, selling piccolos and cornets and sheet music. On Saturdays she plays the French horn in the Salvation Army Band. Her hands always carry the vague scent of brass.

'Have you rung?' Jeannie's mother asks with a nod to the door. Marie shakes her head, and wipes her fingers on her sandwich bag. You must ring the bell to enter the wedding dress shop, a ploy to deter those who want to come in and try on fancy dresses for a bit of frivolity on a dull afternoon.

Miss Crank unbolts the door and delivers a professional smile. 'Hello, hello,' she says, and beckons them inside. She has the voice of a telephone switchboard operator, and a tape measure around her neck, and together they bring her an air of precision. 'Call me Thelma,' she will always say, but her air of crisp formality seems to demand a starchier title. She is the last in a long line of dressmaking Cranks, a well-polished nutmeg of a woman in her mid-forties, with dyed black hair and thick foundation. Eyeshadow has settled into her lids, like a horizon line.

She was married once, to a Mr Powell who owned a furniture store out towards Lytham St Anne's. Everyone in town knows the story. Within months of their marriage she was back at home, humiliated by her new husband's entanglement with a local barmaid. She divorced Mr Powell, retrieved her maiden name and swiftly resumed her role in the family business, never to speak of the matter again.

'Now then!' She claps her hands together lightly as she looks over the assembled group. 'Jeannie, bridesmaids, mother! How are we all? Coffee?' she asks and disappears behind a curtain, into a back room where a kettle blusters.

Dresses line the room like ladies at a tea dance. Dannielle runs her hand slowly along the silks and taffetas. 'Look at this one!' she gulps, tugging out a maroon velvet bodice and pulling a face. 'Would you ever get married in that?' Jeannie smiles thinly. She feels a little sick. It is very warm in the shop, and the wallpaper, all peachy-pink stripes and a border of flowers in full bloom, is making her dizzy. She sits down in a velveteen armchair and looks at her dress hanging behind the counter in a clear plastic cover, next to it the two lilac bridesmaids' dresses and a box containing her mother's hat.

Miss Crank brings cups of milky instant coffee, half-dissolved granules still dancing on the surface, and a plate of pink wafer biscuits. 'So, Jeannie,' she says, in a special voice she reserves for the bride, 'not long now, is it? We'll have this fitting and then one more, just before the wedding. A lot of brides,' she whispers to Jeannie's mother, 'drop a whole dress size the week before the wedding. It's the stress.' Jeannie's mother nods. 'Jeannie dear,' says Miss Crank, 'perhaps you'd like to pop into the changing room and slip out of your clothes. Keep your bra and panties on. I'll come and help you into your dress when you're ready.'

Behind the brocade curtain of the changing room, Jeannie hangs up her anorak and kicks off her shoes. She fights her way out of the pink floral dress, too tight now across the bust and the shoulders, and pulls down her tights, clouding up dust as she yanks them over her feet. It feels more like a medical examination than a dress fitting. She stands before the mirror in her underwear, looking pale and weary and grey.

'Ready, dear?' Miss Crank calls, and tugs back the curtain. The dress is not quite how she remembers it to be, though for weeks now she has been trying to picture it: cream, with capped sleeves, sweetheart neckline and full skirt. The day she chose it, this dress had seemed an acceptable compromise between the overblown confections her mother craved, and the simpler designs she wanted. Now it seems fussier and shinier than she remembered: the trim on the neckline, the rosette at the base of the bodice.

'So, Jeannie, you're going to lift your arms above your head, as if you were about to dive into a swimming pool,' says Miss Crank. Jeannie lifts her arms, closes her eyes and holds her breath. She hears the rustle of the dress as it is lifted, feels its net skirts scratch as they fall down her back, and the soft woomph as they hit the carpet. The fabric smells crisp and new and synthetic. 'There we are, dear,' Miss Crank says, easing up the zip. Jeannie opens her eyes and sees herself full-length in the mirror. She puts her hand to her mouth to smother the rising nausea.

'I'll get your veil,' says Miss Crank, and behind the curtain, Jeannie hears the thump of her heels across the carpet, the soar of her voice telling her mother she looks 'Beautiful! Like a proper bride ...' In the mirror Jeannie does not see a bride at all, just the same plain face, the same thin frame wrapped in a ridiculous cream dress that rustles as she breathes. She touches the skirt, the bodice, the sleeves; she lifts up the train and feels the netting. She closes her eyes again. When they were little, she and Dannielle would dress up in their mother's old clothes, climb into her shoes and clop around the living room. It was easier then to pretend, to make yourself someone else just by stepping into a different dress. They were princesses, secretaries, movie stars. But try as she might today, Jeannie's imagination will not leap to telling her she looks like a bride.

Miss Crank returns with a veil, a tiara and a pair of white high heels. She slides the veil's comb into Jeannie's hair, and adds the little tiara. 'Pop into the heels dear, and then we'll take a look,' says Miss Crank, shuffling open a tub of dressmaking pins. 'How does it feel?' she asks.

'Fine,' says Jeannie. 'I mean, weird ... but fine.'

Miss Crank smiles. 'Well, it will feel a little odd at first. It's not every day we wear a dress this big, is it? Now, I'm just going to take it in a little round the bodice. Lift your arms for me and stay very still.'

Miss Crank is so close Jeannie can smell the milky coffee on her breath. She is holding pins in her mouth and squinting at the waist of the dress. Squinting and pinning, squinting and pinning. It feels hot under the bright lights, and the high heels pinch her toes. Jeannie wishes she could put her arms down. She feels like a music box ballerina, dizzy from all that spinning. 'There!' Miss Crank says after a few moments. 'Now, shall we go out and show your mother?'

The curtain is drawn back and Jeannie shuffles out. The dress crunches as she walks, as if she is crossing gravel, not cheap pink carpet. 'Here she is!' Miss Crank is calling gaily to her mother and Dannielle and Marie. 'Doesn't she look beautiful! There we are, stand on that little box, Jeannie, then everyone can see the skirt. There now, that's how you'll look at the altar.'

'Oh you look gorgeous, love,' her mother says, her voice like a cheap feathered hat, too bright and too perky, and Jeannie sees she has a tissue scrunched in her hand.

Dannielle is standing with her hands on her hips. 'Well, you don't scrub up bad,' she says drily, and everyone laughs. 'Nah, you look lovely, Jeannie,' she grins, and Marie nods.

'You do, you really do. Really beautiful,' she says.

Jeannie looks down at their faces, all starry and pink, and a lump rises in her throat. She fears that she might faint or be sick or burst into tears, such is the swell of forced joviality, the feeling that suddenly every-thing seems too close: the dress too tight, the shop too warm, the room seeming to swing to and fro like a galleon.

'Can I sit down?' she asks in a small voice.

'Oh no, dear,' Miss Crank scolds. 'No sitting. We don't want to get crumpled, do we?'

She smoothes her hand down Jeannie's hip. 'Now. Have you chosen your lingerie yet?'

'Not yet,' says her mother.

'Well, choose something smooth,' Miss Crank says sternly. 'A nice corseted bodice perhaps, because we don't want to spoil the line of the dress. Now, bridesmaids!' She claps her hands and smiles. 'Let's try your dresses, shall we?'

Outside Cranks, the rain is scudding along the street, the wind making tumbleweeds of pie wrappers and cola cans. 'Well,' says her mother, pushing open her umbrella. 'Let's go and get us some lunch.'

The wine bar on King Street is not busy; a few men in suits from the council offices sit smoking, and loosening their ties, while a table of six women laugh loudly over half-empty glasses.

Jeannie's mother puts down the menu. 'I'm going to have the lasagne,' she says firmly. In restaurants, her mother always has the lasagne. When the waiter arrives she speaks to him with the same nervousness she displays when driving. 'We'll all have the lasagne, thank you,' she says, gripping the menu tightly and speaking slightly louder than normal.

'Chips or salad?' he asks, and his pale eyes stay resting on his notepad.

Her mother looks mildly confused. 'Girls?' she asks.

'Chips!' says Dannielle, and makes an attempt to catch the waiter's eye. He looks up and blushes. 'And this white wine,' she adds, pointing at the menu and pouting a little. 'And four glasses.'

The wine is too warm and too sweet, but Jeannie is pleased to find it softens her nausea.

'We came in here the other week,' says Dannielle, looking around.

Marie giggles. 'You came to the wine bar? What for?'

'Thought we'd bag us some rich boyfriends!' Dannielle shuffles her bracelets. 'They was all boring, though,' she laughs. 'And the music was shit.'

Her mother rolls her eyes. 'How's your Stephen?' she asks Marie.

'Oh he's good, yeah,' she smiles. 'Busy, you know? He's been painting the lounge for I don't know how long. I said to him, "Stephen, does it have to be such a ruddy palaver?" I swear we've been sitting on dustsheets for six weeks.'

Jeannie has never been sure what to make of Stephen. He is tall and vague-looking and used to be the quiet boy in her biology class at school. In fact the only real conversation she remembers having with him was when they had to dissect a pig's heart and he told her he liked Marie. The air was thick with the smell of cold, dead meat. He held the scalpel over the left ventricle, and she noticed his hand was shaking.

'I'll tell her,' she said, and wrote the words mitral valve, chordae tendineae, papillary muscle, in calm, neat letters in her exercise book.

After they got engaged, she asked Marie what she liked about Stephen, and she just said she liked having him about. Now he works for the Gas Board and plays snooker at the weekends and thinks about painting the lounge. Whenever she calls round to see Marie he sits staring at the television in silence.

'He's done well for himself, your Stephen,' her mother is telling Marie. 'I saw him the other day in the chippy – did he tell you? – and he did look dishy in his uniform.'

'Mam, he's a gas man, not a fireman!' Dannielle and Marie burst out laughing.

Her mother blushes. 'Well he looks a damned sight smarter than any of the lads you've dragged home, Dannielle,' she says. 'And God only knows whether Jimmy'll scrub that engine oil off his hands in time for the wedding.'

'Oh I don't know,' says Marie, her face pink with the wine. 'He's a nice bit of rough, is Jimmy.'

Jeannie laughs. 'You only see the rough after a while though, eh? Not so much of the nice bit.'

'Try twenty-five years of marriage, Jeannie, then you'll know what rough is!' Her mother is a little giddy now, her head wobbling and her shell earrings jiggling as she talks. 'Your father used to be as sweet as can be. Yes he did,' she nods. 'I was working up at Gaskell's then, and he would come and meet me outside the gate with his hair all combed and his shoes all shined and … is that wine finished, Dannielle?'

The lasagne arrives. 'Plates is hot,' says the waiter, trying not to look at Dannielle. 'D'you want owt else? Vinegar or anything?'

'We'll have another bottle of wine, thank you,' says her mother. 'What was I saying, Jeannie?'

'You were saying "is that wine finished",' Jeannie smiles.

'No, before that … Oh, about your father …' she swallows the warm dregs of her glass, 'he used to pick me up outside the gates on a Friday and he'd buy me a fish supper …'

As her mother talks, Jeannie's thoughts drift to Danny. She will not see him at the station tonight. She imagines him wiping down the tables and rearranging the magazines as he waits for her to arrive. She imagines his blue eyes watching the door and his freckled fingers drumming the counter.

In recent weeks, she has taken to heading up to the station on Monday evenings too. This Monday she found him leaning against the counter reading a book called *Consider the Oyster*. He said he found it in the library. She picked it up and flicked through it while he brewed the tea.

'Have you ever eaten an oyster?' she asked him.

'Of course,' he said.

She scrunched up her face with disgust. 'But they're alive!' she said in a horrified whisper.

Danny slid his eyes left and right, and leaned over the counter. 'I know!' he whispered back.

She laughed, and walked over to the magazines. 'What do they taste like then?' she asked. She stood on her tiptoes and pulled down one of the pornographic magazines from the top shelf.

'Like seawater, and metal,' he said, pouring the milk. 'And they taste kind of slippery.'

'Ugh!' she grimaced. 'That's disgusting. Why would you want to eat that?'

'Well,' he said, and raised an eyebrow, 'they're an aphrodisiac, aren't they?'

'Oh,' she blushed, and put the magazine back on the shelf. Then after an embarrassed silence added: 'Who looks at porn on trains anyway?'

He pushed her cup of tea across the counter. 'They live in brackish water mostly, where it's salty but not as much as sea water,' he said, steering the conversation back to safer territory. 'In Norfolk they live in the salt marshes, and you can just pick them from the beds.'

'You mean you take them while they're sleeping?'

He nodded solemnly. 'You steal them from their beds and eat them alive.'

'You're a monster!' she giggled.

He smiled, and folded his arms. 'Well then, you'd better be nice to me, young lady.'

She had wanted to tell him she wouldn't be there on Thursday, but maybe he wouldn't even miss her; maybe he wouldn't notice. And anyway, she thought, then he might have asked where she would be instead, and she would have had to tell him about the dress-fitting and the wedding. And for some reason she had not quite resolved, she really did not want to tell him about the wedding. She consoled herself with the thought that it wasn't as if she were lying or cheating, it was just something she had failed to mention. But in truth her belly twisted uneasily with the knowledge that they had known each other for two whole months and she still had not told him she would soon be getting married.

Dannielle's voice bursts in shrilly. She is halfway through an anecdote about a customer at the salon who cries every time they cut her hair. It is a story Jeannie has heard before. 'I'm not kidding!' Dannielle nods furiously.

'Every bloody time!' Marie is laughing, and her eyes are wet.

'Tell them about the time she had her legs waxed,' says Jeannie.

'Oh my God!' screeches Dannielle. 'She made us call an ambulance!'

They drink more white wine and they order chocolate fudge cake and it arrives with great foamy skirts of cream and they drink sweet milky coffees and more wine. It is almost six o'clock by the time they call a minicab, her mother long ago too drunk to drive home.

'Jeannie, are you all right, love?' her mother asks. 'Roll down the window, Dannielle.'

She can feel the car upholstery against her legs, the smell of the minicab air freshener swinging from the rear-view mirror, and the sound of the controller's voice crackling through the radio: 'Hall Green, Birch Green, Upholland … Hall Green, Birch Green, Upholland …' Cold air flushes in through the window. Her face feels flabby and strange.

'Is she OK?' the cabby asks. His voice is thick and Scouse and anxious. 'D'you want me to pull over?'

'She's fine,' says her mother. 'Jeannie love, d'you want us to pull over?'

With some effort she nods, and she feels the car slowing to a halt, her mother opening the door and easing her out. 'All right, love, that's all right, you've just had a bit too much to drink, that's all.'

Out in the evening air it is cold and damp and refreshing. The minicab hugs the verge, engine humming, indicator blinking. Jeannie sits down heavily on the edge of the kerb, puts her head between her knees and begins to cry, the hot bewildered tears of the drunk and unhappy.

'All right, Jeannie love.' Her mother rubs her back gently. 'It's all right, we'll be home soon. Take some deep breaths.'

'I don't want to get married, Mam,' she says, the words lumbering forth from her mouth unsteadily. She clutches her head as if to straighten her thoughts. Cars swish by. Her head swims. She begins to sob, great heaves of saliva and mucus and petroleumed air.

'Yes you do, Jeannie love, it's just nerves talking, that.' Her mother strokes her hair. 'Just nerves. Nerves and the wine.'

'No.' Jeannie shakes her head wildly. 'I don't love him, I don't love him, I don't ...' She retches and a wet spray of wine and lasagne and chocolate cake splashes on to the tarmac, she watches it wriggle through the roadside dust. Drizzle falls pleasantly against her clammy cheeks, and for a moment she feels calm. 'I don't love him,' she whispers to the wet road, and her stomach churns. Her mother holds back her hair. 'There you are, love,' she says softly, 'you'll feel better in a minute.'

CHAPTER SIX

Six a.m., and the kitchen stirs with the smell of the electric hob warming, the reassuring odour of cold air sniffing hot metal. The kettle sits on the back ring, ruffling its feathers and making a slow chuckle and cluck. There are no voices at this hour, just the music of routine: the retrieval of teacups from draining-boards, cutlery drawers sliding open and shut, the jolt as the refrigerator door opens, and the soft kiss as it closes. Through the kitchen window the morning trickles across the dark sky as milk into strong tea, and a blackbird stands on the back fence, still and neat and watching.

This evening, they have an appointment with the local priest at St Joseph's, and as Jeannie leans against the kitchen counter, she feels a rush of cold panic rising up from her bare feet. Perhaps Father Michael will be able to smell the creeping, invisible doubt she feels, as a canary sniffs the air and sways in the mine. A hangover is niggling at her forehead, and her throat feels scratchy from last night's sickness. She wishes she were sure she wanted to get married, sure she loved him. She wishes love were like a counterfeit note you could hold up to the light and declare a fake, a thing you could duck in the river to see if it would float. The bridal magazines do not talk about love; they talk about veils and seating plans and sugared almonds. And when she turns the pages of the *Evening Post* to find the photographs of all the newly-weds, the couples smile out with a dogged, freeze-framed certainty she simply does not feel.

When Jimmy proposed she said yes. She said yes in the same way one might agree to parmesan on one's spaghetti – with no wish to cause a fuss or offence. She said yes simply because it is what you are supposed to say in that situation. Because for most girls a wedding always seemed a when, not an if. There was one summer she remembers quite clearly, sitting on the school playing field, patent shoes nudging mounds of mown grass and Nicola Cooper in a pink gingham summer dress, folding her arms and declaring: 'When I get married, I'm going to have a horse and carriage and six bridesmaids, like my Auntie Barbara.' Nicola Cooper works in the chip shop now. She sees her some days, pushing a pram along Golborne Avenue, bleach in her hair and no ring on her finger.

Jimmy is in the shower, the hot-water heater singing through the house, the smell of cheap shower gel spilling through the open bathroom door. Jeannie dresses briskly and is out on the street, unfinished, buttoning up her uniform and smoothing her hair back into its ponytail as the morning spits on her hands. On the bus she sits next to a milk-faced man reading the *Racing Post*. He smells of wet dog. 'Mornin',' he says, and she nods, unzips her anorak and takes out her make-up bag. In the small square of her compact mirror her face stares back, pale and bleak. She rubs concealer beneath her eyes, curls her lashes, streaks blue shadow across her lids. She circles her lips with red liner, colours in the middle, presses a tissue to her mouth. And then she sits, with this bright new weight on her face, her nostrils full of the scent of newspaper ink, Coty lipstick and canine grease.

The morning trails by. People stick their fingers in pots of luxury face cream, they let you tell them what rouge would work best with their complexion, they sniff body creams and talcum powders, and then they drift off in search of the cafeteria and a cup of tea. At half past twelve Jeannie is standing at the counter, sniffing a bottle of eau de cologne, trying to muster an opinion about its blend of white floral head notes, breathing in the narcissus, freesia, magnolia as they settle to a musky base.

'Hey, perfume girl!' She looks up and sees Danny in his felt cap and wool jacket. 'Dinner-time?' he asks, and grins.

As they stroll through the town, she appraises him from the corner of her eye. She likes the way the hems of his blue trousers are wet and the way he walks, with his hands thrust into his jacket pockets and his collar turned up. There is a slight crease in the peak of his cap, and a trail of stubble on his top lip that makes him look a little dishevelled. They are walking close enough that she can smell him, warm, like boot polish and toast.

'What?' he asks eventually.

'What what?' she asks.

'Why've you been looking at me like that ever since we left Pemberton's?'

She shrugs shoulders, her anorak rustles. 'Dunno,' she says, and he smiles and her face grows hot.

The municipal park was built in the summer of 1878. It lies just beyond the town centre, almost thirty acres of lawns and duck ponds and avenues, of flower beds in fiercely jubilant colours hemmed in by low, looping metal fences. In early spring, the council dispatches teams of men in matching green sweaters, heads down in the spitting rain, planting rows of low-blooming flowers: red and orange non-stop begonias, ageratum 'Champion Blue', helichrysum 'Silver Mist', bacopa, dichondra 'Red Dragon's Wings', marigolds, salvias, acmella oleracea

'Peek-a-boo', red and white impatiens. In the spring, red and yellow tulips sit suddenly bolt upright and waxy. But by midsummer they are sagging, splayed and weary, like aged women swooning in the afternoon heat.

Along the main parade stands a brass statue of a local MP, Sir Francis Maugham, erected by public subscription in 1886, and all verdigrised now, save for his right toe, which park-goers touch for luck as they pass. A few steps along is an ornate fountain, dry for decades; today, its stone basin holds a layer of brown scum and twigs and a red and yellow McDonald's straw. There is a bowling green, a sandpit, a plastic slide and two swings rattling about in the wind. On the back lawn squats the boarded-up bandstand; loose chipboard unveils the smell of piss and damp that lurks inside. After school, kids climb in and smoke cigarettes, try to light fires that never catch in the wet air. Down among the leaves lie empty cider cans and ice-pop wrappers, the faint scent of matches. In the brief moment between childhood and puberty, the boys in this town lust after fire; they burn insects and branches and school books. Sometimes they burn down entire schools. The park's pavilions and parades, its railings and its awnings have all been painted and repainted every couple of years, layer atop layer, like the girl with bad skin wearing too much make-up. And so the park appears awkward and frumpy, overdone in the middle of the day, as if hoping, despite it all, that someone might ask it to dance.

Parks like this sprang up all over the North in the nineteenth century; they were built for the workers, gifts from the aristocracy, wasteland groomed into civility, in an attempt to impose an ordered morality, a green-leafed buffer against the wanton sprawl of the poor. After all, there were no gardens among the rows of factory terraces, just a clatter of back doors, coal sheds, yards, alleyways. When they arrived, the municipal parks, with their turkey oaks and bhutan pines, their ponds and pavilions, proved a popular weekend destination for the people of the town. But things change. In the 1970s the warm glow of the television drew them back indoors. And now the parks sit unused, like the front room, and the best cruet.

There are few people in the park this lunchtime. Mothers and toddlers come to feed the ducks; elderly couples out for a stroll, he in a cap, she in a rainscarf. The trees are bare, clawing at the white sky with its pale winter sun, and the afternoon looks cold and starkly lit, like an empty refrigerator.

They walk along the main parade and up the broad steps leading to the pavilion tea room. There are forty steps, she counts them as they climb, and they are all smooth and dark and in the middle they dip softly, as if performing a deferential curtsey before the grand old dame of the pavilion. The pavilion is unquestionably the *pièce de résistance* of the park: an elaborate octagonal building perching atop a slight hill, it has three tiers of pale stone and deep red brick, above which sits a glass dome, ornate and frilly, like a charlotte russe, towering precariously above the conifers. Looked at objectively, the pavilion is a majestic structure, a striking example of Victorian architecture, but its beauty is marred by bottle-green paintwork and a general air of defeat, as if it has taken to wearing its housecoat all day and drinking gin at breakfast-time.

Some years ago, a tea room was opened in its lower level. By anyone's standards it was something of a half-hearted enterprise that made most of its money selling choc-ices in the summer months. Yet it remains open all year round, hardy and resilient, despite the fact that in the wintertime its customers are few and far between, and the only warmth is from a small electric heater that judders in the corner.

Inside, the ceiling is low and the walls are the colour of packet cake-mix. There are seven tables that stand in rather careless formation and entirely fail to fill the room. Upon closer inspection it is apparent that they are mismatched cast-offs from the local comprehensive school, and as such are stained with ink, with the names of various ex-students carved deep into their grey Formica. The chairs are from elsewhere, a community centre or a day-care facility perhaps, with thin black metal legs and orange plastic seats; the kind of chairs that long to be stacked. In the middle of the floor today a bright red bucket sits atop a copy of yesterday's *Evening Post*, and into its belly the roof drips a steady plut-plut-plut, as if distilling the very essence of the pavilion itself.

What redeems the tea room is its elegant windows that stare out over the park to the thick rhododendron bushes by the railway track, and to the gatehouse, and the old cotton works beyond. It is not a bad town from this height: low-lying, slightly cowed beneath the weather, with endless rows of terraces for the rain to run along, and in the distance the sweep of moorland and fields.

It is not busy. A thin, elderly couple sitting with sweet tea and a crossword, and a burly man in overalls who has spread an Ordnance Survey map across the tabletop and is pulling at his bottom lip with dirty finger and thumb. Along the far wall runs the counter with its great silver urn, and its scones trapped under clingfilm. Behind the counter is a sign in black felt-tip: *Sandwitches — ham, egg, cheese, meat paste*. And slightly to the left stands a woman of about fifty, with short curly hair, dyed a savage shade of red. Her face is shiny and flushed, and her cleavage so creased it resembles a pink Spanish fan. 'Yes, love,' she says, and places her stubby fingers on the counter.

Danny surveys the refrigerator with its dusty cans of pop, sausage rolls and tubs of cheap margarine. 'I'll have a pie and a cup of tea, and she'll have … What'll you have?'

'Are you buying me my dinner?'

'I know how to treat a lady,' he says, and smiles in a lop-sided kind of way, so that the woman behind the counter glows pinker and says 'Go on, love, let 'im treat yer!'

'Well, I'll have an egg barm then. And a tea. Thanks.'

'No barms, love,' the woman says sadly. 'I've got white sliced and that's all today.'

'White's fine,' Jeannie nods, and watches the woman's meaty hands find plates and knives and teacups.

They sit by the window, where the breeze sneaks in round the glass.

'How's the station?' she asks.

'Oh it's, y'know …' He sips his tea. 'Well, there's a rush on hot chocolate. That keeps me busy.'

'I'll bet.'

'You looked pretty run off your feet there yourself in the perfume hall,' he smiles.

'Yep. Mad, it's been mad, mad busy. I think we're in danger of running out of scent, in fact.'

'Really? And how many bottles have you sold today?'

'Oh let me see,' she says, and stares at the ceiling, as if engaged in complex mental arithmetic. 'Absolutely none at all,' she concludes eventually, and bites firmly into her sandwich.

'I missed you last night,' he says suddenly, and fiddles with his teacup. 'I mean, no big deal or anything, I was just worried …'

'I'm sorry,' she says quietly. 'I had something I had to do. A family thing.'

'Oh it's no big deal,' he says again. 'It's just … I was worried, and I'd saved you some cherry cake.' She smiles, and he blushes. 'I gave it to my grandad. I was telling him about you, about how you watch the trains and stuff, cos he used to work on the railways …'

He's gabbling a little now, as if trying to scuff over his confession, play it down, and Jeannie feels a peculiar tightness in her chest, as if she wants to cry or to laugh and so she says abruptly: 'Does it get weird living with your grandad ever?'

'Nah,' he says gustily, relieved by the change in conversation. 'I like it. He keeps his house really neat, and he does things people don't bother to do any more, like … before he goes to bed, he puts out all his breakfast stuff for the morning, his teacup and that. You can set your watch by him.'

She smiles. 'What's he like, your grandad?'

'He looks like me,' he grins. 'Or I look like him. When he was young. He's proper dapper though. Shines his shoes and that. And he wears a vest. And he kind of whistles a bit when he talks. I like that.' He grins again. He has nice teeth, sort of small and crooked, but friendly-looking.

'What about your grandma?'

'I don't remember her much. I remember how she smelled, you know? Like talc, and kind've like soap. I've seen pictures of her. There's this one of her at the seaside, and you can tell it's windy, and she doesn't know whether to hold on to her hat or hold down her skirt and she's grinning at the camera, at my grandad, and you can tell she loves him. They got married when they were seventeen. She died though. She had a stroke, you know? One Christmas Eve. I saw her in the hospital; they'd taken her teeth out and she had all these tubes, and there was this big bruise down the side of her face where she'd hit the carpet when she fell. He took her some flowers, some carnations, and she fucken hated carnations, but they were all he could get, you know? He kept saying 'I'm sorry about the carnations, Gladys. I'm sorry about the flowers, love,' and pressing her hand. And then she died. They were married for forty years.'

'That's awful,' she says, and immediately regrets it, as if her words swab at something much bigger and wetter than they can hope to mop up.

'Yeah. He had us, and his friends, and his shed and the radio and that, but it's not the same, is it? You've shared a bed with someone all those years. I mean, he didn't know how to make the bed, you know? He didn't know where she kept the iron, or how to wash the sheets. He took them to the launderette, and there's all these old dears clucking round him, and it's … well, it's fine now. It's fine. He's fine. Kept all her stuff though.'

'Really?' She is pulling the crusts off her sandwich.

'Yeah. All her dresses and her hats and that. What about yours?'

'Nan lives on our street,' she says. 'She's my mum's mum. And my Nana Mary lives two streets down. I never met my grandad, but she's got her bloke, Brian – she calls him her fancy man, but they've been together twenty years. He wears a wig.'

Danny smirks. 'Now that is fancy.'

'Isn't it just? And he has a place in Tenerife, a time-share y'know. He wears too much aftershave and he plays golf, but I guess he makes her happy.'

'I don't think my grandad thought about meeting someone else. I asked him about it once, cos the woman from the launderette was always popping round with her lipstick on, you know? But he said he'd married the best woman he ever met, and he married her for life ...' He laughs. 'He said "Danny, I'm like a swan."'

'You mean your grandad can break a man's arm?'

'Yeah. That's right. He may be seventy-one, but he's tough. And he's wily.'

'Do you believe in that?'

'The arm-breaking thing?'

'No, I mean the marrying for life thing.'

'Yeah, of course. I mean my mum and dad got divorced, and I guess it was for the best. Or they didn't try. Or whatever. But I don't want to be like them, you know. Why, don't you?'

'I don't know,' she says, and her eyes sharpen. 'I think marriage is hard. I think all you can do is try really hard and hope it works out, and sometimes it won't.'

He looks at her for a moment, tearing up the sandwich crusts with her fingers. 'That's a pretty bleak winter there, little bird. Don't you want some Prince Charming to ride in and sweep you off your feet?'

'Yeah,' she says quietly. 'Of course. But I'm not a daft little girl. That stuff doesn't happen. Not really, and not round here. And anyway, princes are a bit thin on the ground these days.' She throws him a withering little smile. He wants to touch her hand, but instead he grips his teacup.

'Danny?' she asks. 'When you do something, like, anything big, how sure should you be that it's what you want to do?'

He looks up, mouth full of pie and raises his eyebrows sharply. 'Like what?'

She frowns. 'I dunno … Like when you moved here. Did you know it was the right thing to do? Did you ever think maybe you weren't sure, and maybe you should move somewhere else?'

He swallows slowly. 'Nah,' he shakes his head. 'I liked it here, you know? I knew I liked it. And I knew my grandad was here. And I knew I could get a room. And it just felt right. Why, what's the matter?'

'I dunno,' she says. 'I just don't know what I want to do.'

'What, when you grow up?'

'Yeah,' she laughs, and presses her teacup against her face. 'D'you know when that'll be?'

Rain hits the window. 'Bloody hell!' cries the tea-room woman and rushes out from behind the counter to reposition the bucket. They stand at the window, watching it thrash against the steps, watching their pale reflections bobbing in the glass.

'We're going to be late!' Jeannie whispers, half worried, half excited.

'Good!' Danny whispers back.

You can see the raindrops hitting the pond, gathering in the soft dip of the steps, sliding down the gutter. It stops abruptly.

'Shall we?' he asks, and they head out into the cold air.

The park is shining wet, its colour heightened, like the face of someone who has just stopped crying. Above them the sky is shifting, dark clouds, sudden sunshine, back again, and beneath their feet the path is soft and damp, pale gravel smudging against their shoes. There is no one else to be seen on the parade. Sir Francis Maugham shines brilliant green in his verdigris coat. Danny rubs his toe as they pass.

'It's going to rain again,' she says. 'You can smell it.'

'Yeah,' he laughs, 'that's what I wished for.'

The drops fall plumply, heavily, rolling down their

collars and under their coats. Jeannie pulls up her anorak hood.

He grabs her hand. 'Come on,' he says, and ducks into the rhododendron bush.

It smells of wet earth, of mulching leaves and bones and feathers and curls of rotting tree bark. The rain putters against the waxy leaves, and from somewhere up high a bird sings out wild and shrill and happy. He slides his hand up to her face, rough fingertips brushing against her cheek, against her forehead, smoothing her wet fringe, pushing her hood back, and he kisses her, all lips and bristles and the smell of the tea room. She runs her hands along his pale wrists, to the cuff of his jacket, up to his shoulders, to the nape of his neck, presses her cold body against his, kisses a long, certain-lipped kiss.

Father Michael is a man washed pale: wan-framed, with fine ginger hair and watery blue eyes. He sits in the presbytery living room thinking of crumpets, of the tray now being set out in the pantry by Mrs McCusker, a faded woman who has been loyally in his service for fifteen years, yet he could not tell you the colour of her hair. Father Michael is a creature of routine, contented by the gentle rhythm of the clock in the hallway and the sound of the choir rehearsing next door, as they do every Thursday evening, their voices pressing through the paint and the plasterboard.

The young couples come and go, ebbing and flowing, as if brought in by the tide. He had christened these two. And confirmed them. It said so on the filing card he gripped in his right hand, and whose inky-blue scrawl caused him to squint.

'Well,' he says, looking up at their nervous faces, 'June 14th, is it?'

'That's right, Father,' Jimmy says in his church voice, somewhat lower and humbler than his usual tone.

The purr of the gas fire fills the room, and Father Michael gropes around for the usual words. 'Well,' he says again. 'I expect you are both very excited to be getting married.' He looks at the girl, who seems rather terrified. 'And probably a little nervous too,' he adds, to reassure her. 'The thing to remember is that marriage is a partnership, a union blessed by God ...' he trails off and for want of a conclusion, adds a cough.

'I expect you won't be wanting the full mass?' he asks, and the couple nods. Nobody does these days. And if he is honest, he is rather glad. 'And so we just need to choose the readings,' he continues, 'and the hymns, of course.' He half-stands, opens a drawer, takes out a manila folder. Inside is a sheaf of A4 photocopies, and he hands a copy to the young couple, whose names he has already forgotten. 'So you must take a look at this, and choose ... well, all the instructions are there. And then you must let me know what you have chosen so we can, you know, rev up the choir and things.' He smiles vaguely. The girl still looks worried.

'The marriage service is a serious commitment,' Father Michael says gently, 'but of course it is also an opportunity to celebrate your love for one another before those you love and also before God. It is a happy day.' He pauses, smiles, rises to his feet and shepherds them to the door. 'Of course, should you have any concerns ... well, you know where to find me,' he says as he lifts the latch.

The cold March night rushes in, and with it the glow of the streetlights and the distant swish of buses. 'Goodbye,' he says, and holds out his hand, soft-skinned and lukewarm to the touch. They trip down the steps, out on to the drive, and he rests on the latch a moment and watches the young couple drift towards the road: quiet steps, heads bowed, their bodies some distance apart. In the space between them he sees the last of the day's light, a pale strip above the trees, bare branches scumbling the sky. The days are getting longer, he thinks to himself; it would not be so very long till June. He feels the warmth of the hallway press against his calves and slowly he closes the presbytery door. 'Mrs McCusker?' he calls.

CHAPTER SEVEN

The room smelled stale, as if the window had not been opened in a very long time, and a glass of half-drunk orange squash sat on the ledge, its contents fading to a surly shade of amber. All across the dressing table spilled cassettes, records, chewing-gum wrappers, there were T-shirts straggling across the carpet, and a damp bath towel draped over the corner of the wardrobe door. But the heavy furniture gave the room an air of formality; wardrobe, dressing table, chair, standing discreetly against the wall, like waiters to be beckoned.

Danny lay on his belly, breathed the greasy pillow air, and after a few minutes slid his arm down to the slim dusty space between the bed and the table and fished out a paperback novel. Lately he had begun a programme of manly self-improvement which principally involved teaching himself to appreciate neat whisky, jazz records and the novels of Charles Bukowski.

He rolled on to his back, crossed his ankles and inspected the cover. *Women*, it was called; the word was printed in sturdy black letters above an illustration of a finely turned ankle. It had been with some pride that he had taken this book out of the local library; it implied, he felt, a worldly wisdom, an acquaintance with both the work of subversive American writers and a certain familiarity with the opposite sex. The cover alone suggested an appreciation of the female form. He traced his finger along her calf. Outside he could hear the sound of his grandfather digging in the garden, the cold, flinty strike of the shovel, and the birds singing the sad, damp song of early evening. He curved back the book cover so the spine flinched and cracked. 'I was naturally a loner,' he read, 'content just to live with a woman, eat with her, sleep with her, walk down the street with her. I didn't want conversation, or to go anywhere except the race-track or the boxing matches.'

Danny paused and considered the idea. It sounded a rather noble existence. He pictured himself, a strong, solitary figure who began each morning with the cold scrape of the razor blade, a glass of milk and a roll-up cigarette smoked on the back step, a man who kept himself to himself and didn't waste his afternoons in the pub drinking stout and talking football. Horses and fighting, those were the real sports. He warmed to the idea and began to picture, too, all the women who would try to change him, flitting around him with their frills and their fussing. But he would resist, he would keep his life pared right down to the rind, he would keep his house smelling like a man's house; no lavender water, cut flowers, potpourri in his home, just the scent of shoe polish and tobacco, coffee and last night's supper.

He settled the book against his chest. Next week, he decided, he would go to the bookies or to a boxing match. He imagined himself, arms folded, chewing a matchstick, while in the ring two brawny men rained punches, spat in buckets, shuffle-danced across the floor, as their hair clung sweatily to their scalps.

He had only once been in a proper fight himself. In the days after Tina had found she was pregnant, when the whole world had seemed to rear up violently in front of him, her father had collared him outside the chip shop. Frank was a bulky man; not tall, not even especially wide, but there was something gristly about him, something fierce and furious. It was there in the way he had gripped Danny's collar, swung him around, and thrown his slight body against the brick wall of the chip shop. Danny had felt as if he were on a fairground waltzer, breathless, a little sick, but somehow electrified.

He had offered up his face and let Frank hit him.

He could remember it now: the collision of knuckles and face, the unfamiliar pressure against his teeth, and with it the sudden warm shock of blood that filled his mouth, his nose, that ran down his throat. And in those moments, as he half-closed his eyes, saw the streetlights dancing and twirling, he pictured the scene, his slim young shoulders thrust against the glossy red brick, splayed beneath those heavy punches. He pictured the blood that arced so gracefully from his lip, over his pale T-shirt and fell into the dust, bright and brilliant among the chip wrappers and the empty cola bottles. And caught up a little in the drama of the event, he had perhaps feigned more pain than in truth he actually felt, because as he hit the pavement, as the gravel scuffed his face and he came to rest on the cool black asphalt, he rather liked the idea of himself as the noble, broken hero of the story.

He lifted the book, read over the sentence again, but his thoughts returned to Tina. He could see her, with her sandy hair and her freckled shoulders, and the blue eyes she scrunched up in the sunshine. When he thought of Tina he always thought of her strawberry lipgloss, of how he could taste it when he kissed her, and smell it on her breath, and how when he held her hand, her right index finger was always slightly sticky with it. He preferred to picture her this way, the way she was when they first met, not how she was at the end, sour-faced and sharp-tongued, her eyes taking on the same brittle look as her mother's.

He stared at the ceiling, at the ripples of Artex and the long grey frond of cobweb clinging to the lightshade, and he fell to thinking of Jeannie's face: plain, mild-eyed, a face so lightly flavoured that it seemed to evaporate before its taste ever really came into focus. He viewed her as an experiment of sorts; she was so unmoulded, he almost felt as if with the barest of effort he could shape her features into a different kind of face altogether.

There were flashier girls he might have chosen. The blonde in the ticket office, for instance, who he'd kissed one boozy Friday night at the Seven Stars, more out of inquisitiveness than desire, out of a vague sense that if you unsettled the universe something interesting might happen. Of course all that did happen was that the girl proceeded to moon over him until a week or two later he eventually relented and took her out for a drink, and she sat there, in a low-cut blouse, her lipstick coming off on the rim of her glass, sipping her schnapps and lemonade and giggling until he took her into the car park and undid her blouse just to bring the evening to a close. He'd buried his face in her neck, just to avoid her lips, and now he remembered her perfume, heavy and sweet and tropical, entirely out of place in that puddly, windswept yard. After that he couldn't be doing with her.

In his short time in the town he had acquired a number of admirers, and often he passed his journey to work by counting through their names, like stations on the line. Susan in the bakery; Pauline, the barmaid at the Crown; several of the morning regulars in the station café; Joanne from the bus stop; Elaine in the Spar; and Rita, the female librarian – a bulky woman of about fifty, who wore snug-fitting short-sleeved jumpers, through which pressed the lines of a too-small bra.

Over the last few months he had been conducting an exercise in charming Rita – waving to her as he walked through the turnstile, engaging her in conversation as he checked out his books – always an impressively diverse selection: Friedrich Engels, some Gertrude Stein, a recording of *Madame Butterfly* on cassette. Once, as he renewed a copy of the collected poems of Arthur Rimbaud, he told her that he wrote poetry too. He had watched her face colour as she suggested, breathlessly, that he should perhaps consider attending the library's weekly poetry evening.

Now she often let him take out more than six books. He didn't need more than six books. Sometimes he barely opened them during the course of the week; they just sat on his chest of drawers next to a small brass ornament of the three wise monkeys that his grandmother had bought on a summer holiday to Beer.

He had been to the poetry evenings once or twice. At

the first there was a reading by a man who specialised in Lancashire dialect poems. He was short and rather bulbous-looking, the curve of his belly sitting beneath a thick green jumper. He hitched up his trousers as he sat down, leant one elbow on his knee, cleared his throat and began:

> Thurs a famous seaside place called Blackpool,
> That's noted fur fresh air an' fun,
> An' Mr and Mrs Ramsbottom,
> Went thur with Albert, thur son …

Danny'd looked up and found Rita glancing over in an embarrassed way. He gave her a wink, and she blushed and looked at her lap.

The poet read in an exaggerated accent, flat vowels, short consonants, rolled the r of Ramsbottom extravagantly; he went eeyore-ing his way through the next verse and the next. Danny was close enough to catch the scent of his breath: a sour, milky smell like manure. This was what he hated about the North: this languishing in regionality, this eeh-by-gumming and hotpot suppers, while over there, just yards from where they were sitting, were rows of proper poetry books no one would ever read.

The group applauded. There must have been about eight of them in total, all middle-aged, all balancing their teacups and saucers on their knees, all quietly nibbling their biscuits and laughing on cue. The poet coughed and announced that he would now read a traditional piece entitled the 'Oldham Weaver', and then afterwards he would answer questions from the floor. 'Oi'm a poor cotton-weyver, as mony a one knoowas,' he began.

Oi've nout for t'year, an' oi've word eawt my clooas,
Yo'ad hardly gi' tuppence for aw as oi've on,
My clogs are both brosten, an stuckings oi've none,
Yu'd think it wur hard, To be browt into th' warld,
To be clemmed, an' do th' best as yo' con ...

Danny stifled a yawn and stretched out his legs. He noticed Rita fishing a tissue out of her short jumper sleeve, and he wondered how long it had been tucked up there, beside the soft stretch of skin between her elbow and her armpit. It flattered him that he had succeeding in kindling this crush in her. Sometimes he contemplated asking her out for a drink just to see her flutter, and occasionally he imagined peeling off that fine-knit jumper, to find the thick-strapped lingerie beneath, and the scent of sweat and talcum powder that would rise up from her pale, plump body. In the bag he carried to work, he had a copy of Orwell's *The Road to Wigan Pier* that Rita had given to him once – she told him she had two copies, and what was the point of having a spare?

And when he sniffed the pages they held that same sweet, powdery smell.

'Alan,' a woman across the other side of the circle was saying, 'why do you choose to write in dialect?' Scrawny and prim in a blue polo-neck, as she spoke a pair of spectacles, hanging on a cord around her neck, bobbed lightly against her chest.

Alan folded his arms above his belly, and tucked his palms under his armpits so that only the thumbs poked out, hitching a lift in the direction of his shoulders. 'There is to me no sound more beautiful than Lancashire dialect,' he replied, and around the room they nodded and smiled with approval. 'Addled, alicker, arse o'er tit ...' he said each word carefully, as if testing its weight, 'these words are ambrosia to me. And for me to perform or compose verse ...' he paused, disengaged his right hand from his left armpit and waved it in the air, 'for me to perform or compose verse in any other form of language, well, it would be a fish on a bicycle, that. Unnatural.'

There followed more questions – people wanted to know how he had begun writing, if he wrote every day, what kind of pens he favoured, if he was especially proud of any one of his poems.

Danny shuffled in his chair, rubbed his shoes together. When there was a pause he spoke: 'Alan,' he began, and smiled warmly, 'would you regard yourself as continuing the grand linguistic exploration of that other great English poet Gerard Manley Hopkins?'

In truth, Danny was relying on a vague recollection of a long-ago English Literature lesson that had centred on the study of Hopkins' poem 'Spring', but his strength, he felt, lay in the conviction of his delivery.

Alan coughed and burred a little. 'Well, young man,' he said, and the group looked at him expectantly. Danny stayed quite still, just the lick of a smile on his lips. 'I certainly feel I am conducting an exploration, though whether I can lay claim to continuing the work of this Mr Hopkins of yours I couldn't say — I tend to be suspicious of fellows named Gerard.' He pronounced the name grandly, as if it were a foreign delicacy, and the crowd laughed, and then Alan gave the smile of a man who has just reversed his car into a particularly tricky parking space.

Danny felt vaguely thwarted, but consoled himself with the fact that Rita looked impressed. There was a round of applause for Alan, and the reading drew to a close. The others were lingering, milling around, waiting for books to be signed, and as he headed to the door Danny placed his hand on the small of Rita's back and whispered, 'See you next week.' He felt her tremble under his palm.

He liked this little town, he had thought as he walked out into the cold night. And now as he lay on his back staring up at the ceiling he recalled that sudden rush of warmth he had felt for his adopted home, the feeling that you could spend a lifetime here, rattling contentedly from office job to library readings, to the Ritzy to the pub. You could settle down with a nice girl and spend your whole life on the same bus route. And when he thought of it he felt a sudden wash of calm, the feeling of a man who finally stops struggling and allows himself to sink.

It was different here to the town where he had grown up, though it was only a few stops along. He didn't like to go back if he could help it. He thought of his dad and his new wife and their kids. The house with the red front door. The swing in the scraggy grass. The barbecues where the kids would tear about with the hosepipe, leaping and jumping and shrieking on the wet lawn till they were tired and tearful and it was way past their bedtime. And then late into the night his dad would sit out in the garden, sunburned, drinking lager, morose, while his new wife, mushy on cheap pink wine, would be spilling secrets to a neighbour and crying about something half-forgotten.

He'd leave then, sneak out of the side gate and on to the estate, where the pavements were still warm from the day and it felt as if the air was swarming with a hundred barbecues. He'd take the long route back to his mum's house, along the back roads, past his old school and across the overpass. When he opened the front door he knew he'd find her where he left her, in the lounge, watching the telly, sewing cushion covers with quilted kittens and owls. Her eyes would shift up from the screen. 'Hello, love,' she'd say. 'Nice time?' But her voice was distant and grey and sounded as if it had not been dusted in a very long time.

He worried about his mother. He remembered a time when he was young, when she was bright and boisterous and colourful, a woman who left lipstick on his cheek and a trail of scent wherever she went. This was before they had divorced. His father had often worked away then, and on Friday nights Danny would sit on the end of his parents' bed, watching his mother get dressed up for his return: her hair in rollers, her face slowly taking shape as she sponged on foundation, patted on powder, drew in her eyebrows.

'Make us a G and T, will you, love?' she'd say as she painted her lips, and he would scamper downstairs, thrilled by his mission, pad across the lounge, haul the big green gin bottle from the cabinet, measure it into a tumbler with his finger. Two knuckles deep was how she drank it. The tonic water was prone to fizzing and he would have to unscrew the top slowly; he felt it was a fine art, the unscrewing of a tonic bottle. Then two cubes of ice and a slice of lemon, cut slowly, carefully, with the sharpest knife they owned. And then he would pause and breathe it in, this tall glass of perfume. It was the smell of his mother at night.

Upstairs she was dancing to Steely Dan and unravelling the rollers. 'Aren't you my little star!' she would cry as he walked in, carrying the gin glass in both hands, and her eyes would light up as if he'd won a gameshow prize. She would take a long sip then smile and turn the music up loud, so loud he could feel it in the carpet beneath his feet. 'Dance with your mam!' she'd laugh, and grab his hand, and they'd twirl across the carpet to 'Rikki Don't Lose that Number'.

Later, he would lie in bed, much like now, staring at the ceiling and listening for the engine of his father's car. And when he heard its slow, familiar drone, and the squeal of the loose fan belt as it turned the corner, he would slip out from under the duvet, stand in his bedroom window in his pyjamas, watching for the car to appear along the road and slowly pull up outside the house. He would watch his mother run down the driveway in her heels, clatter to a halt by the driver's door and fling herself against her father as he climbed out. For a long while they would stand there, saying nothing, just holding on.

He imagined his father inhaling the scent of his mother, the perfume dabbed behind her ears, the hairspray, the gin, the waxy, floral fragrance of her lipstick. If he strained he could just about hear the radio still playing on the car stereo, a late-night love hour on some local station, crackling out into the still, suburban night.

Now she never went out. Every night she ate her dinner on her lap in front of the television, microwaveable meals for one, flabby pasta dishes that all tasted the same. The cupboards were full of Penguin biscuits and Mini Rolls, and she never wore perfume or drank gin or curled her hair any more. She didn't listen to Steely Dan and she didn't dance, and just about the only thing she liked to talk about were the television soap operas.

His dad left years ago. One Friday night he just didn't come home. His mother had sat in the lounge, drinking and waiting, and upstairs he had stood in the window for what seemed like for ever, till his legs felt stiff and cold and the sky started to get light. And then he had sneaked through the chilly house, and found his mother asleep on the rug, her hand cupping a glass of whisky. Her face was pale and all her make-up had run down her face, bright-blue eyeshadow, blurred pink lipstick, smudged blusher, trails of mascara and orange foundation; it looked like the picture of bonfire night he had painted the previous November.

She stopped speaking to the neighbours. At the shops she sent him in with her purse and a list of groceries while she sat waiting in the car. She gave up aerobics and PTA meetings and took to staying in and ordering things from catalogues – table nests and ornaments, teapots in the shape of geese, a chain of porcelain elephants for the mantelpiece. There were scented sachets for the drawers, plastic clips for freezer bags, thimbles and guest soaps and enamel signs reading *God Bless This House*. The last time he'd visited he'd noticed she had begun a collection of masks on the wall above the telephone, palm-sized porcelain clowns, with feathers and jewels and empty eyes.

After Tina, after it had all gone wrong and she'd got rid of the baby, got rid of him too and met someone else, he couldn't really think of a reason to stick around. He had a bit of money saved up; he'd counted it all out on his bedroom floor and found there was enough to take him to Paris. And so it was an early morning coach down to Dover, rolling up his sweater and dozing against the window, and then a ferry ride across the Channel and on through the French countryside, which was cold and misty and grey at that time of year.

All the way he listened to his Walkman, to a compilation he had made for Tina but never given to her. The Beatles, Leonard Cohen, Joni Mitchell, Nick Drake, the Beach Boys. Between each song came a muffled clunk as he'd stopped and started the recording. There was a brief snatch of the DJ's voice before the Cure began, and at the end of the first side a song from a children's tape, 'Two Little Boys' which he'd included half to make her laugh and half to win her back. The second side opened with Harry Nilsson singing 'What'll I Do', a record he'd dug out of his parents' record collection in the loft. He rewound the song and played it over. And then again. And again. The coach edged its way into Paris, and he looked out at the streets, grey and rainy and sad, at the cars that jostled and jerked and beeped their horns, and at the cold, foreign faces of all the passers-by who knew nothing about him, or where he was from or the girl that he'd loved who had left him. And then he began to cry.

He had gone to the Eiffel Tower and the Arc de Triomphe. He had visited the Louvre and the Musée D'Orsay. He had walked along the Seine and all around the Père Lachaise cemetery. It had rained constantly, and he had listened to nothing but Harry Nilsson. At night, in his youth hostel bunk, so cold his legs got cramp, he had fallen asleep with his headphones on. On the third morning he piled everything back into his bag, walked to the coach station and caught the first bus back. On the ferry he stayed below deck until they neared Dover and then he rushed to see the land approaching, feeling something warm and sweet fluttering in his chest. At the service station he had bought a sausage sandwich and a cup of tea and flicked through a copy of the *Sun*. Back on the road, he had delighted in the way the green of the land grew deeper, richer as they neared the North.

On his bedside table now he had the little Eiffel Tower

he had bought with his remaining coins, at a tourist stop by the coach station. He claimed it was a memento of his holiday, of the great city of Paris, but really it was a reminder not to stray too far from home.

He'd always liked his grandad. When his parents split up, Grandad would ride over in his little orange Golf, take him to the park or fishing along the canal. When he got back from Paris he'd seen no point in going back to his mother's, and so he got off a few stops early and headed to his grandad's house.

He told himself he was just staying here until he worked out what to do with his life. Just working in the station buffet till something better came along. Just hanging out with Jeannie while he passed the time. He stretched, picked up his book again, and began to read.

CHAPTER EIGHT

Jimmy bowled down the street. Monday morning, just after seven, and the start of the working week. He felt antsy today, a little restless, and as he drove what carried him was the nagging thought that something, somewhere was wrong.

The weather was still unsettled, and through the windscreen the sky shifted uneasily above him. He sat and stared at the traffic lights, stubbornly fixed at red, and tried to work out just what it was that bothered him. He was, by nature and by trade, a mechanically minded man, and as he pulled away from the junction, shifting first to second to third, he took a methodical approach to the problem.

For starters, Jeannie had come home late on Saturday

night. They'd rowed in the pub, of course, and when he had returned home in the early hours and found the bed empty he had assumed she was asleep in the spare room, making some kind of silent protest. But later, when he'd got up to piss, he'd seen her clothes bundled in the hallway and it had struck him as peculiar.

What had they rowed about? He delved into the back of his mind and rooted around in the darkness. It must have been something about the wedding – that was all they ever seemed to talk about lately – in truth, he struggled to recall what they ever talked about before the wedding. God, it could have been anything: his suit, the cake, the DJ, her mother, his mother ... He turned on the radio, let the sound of Bon Jovi fill his head for a while.

Where had she been? Jimmy turned the music down. At her mother's? It seemed unlikely. At Marie's house? It was a possibility, but again strange. Did she know anyone else? He delved further into the darkness and came up with nothing. It had never struck him as strange before, but suddenly it seemed odd that Jeannie had so few friends. Just him. The first heavy sploshes of rain hit the windscreen. He flicked on the wipers and they squealed and screeched, a distant violin practice in the engine. He'd have to fix that.

Then there was the matter of Terri. She was a regular at the Bull, and a bit of a head-turner; buxom and blonde, she wore everything tight and short and low, she drank lager tops and was always chewing gum. She chewed Juicy Fruit, in the bright yellow wrappers, and when you spoke to her, the air between you billowed with synthetic fruit flavour. She'd shuck each stick of gum out of its foil with one hand and then fold it on to her tongue in one smooth moment. 'What's with the gum?' he'd asked her the first night they met. 'I just like to have something in my mouth, Jimmy ...' she'd said, saucily. 'Are you blushing?'

Saturday night, they'd been flirting outrageously in the pub, just a bit of harmless fun, wedged between the bar and the jukebox, but even now he wasn't altogether sure that nothing had happened. He frowned and turned up the radio again, trying to block out the flooding sense of guilt. He had a dim memory of the two of them outside, huddled in a doorway, and he could still feel the soft fabric of her dress beneath his palm.

Girls like Terri made him wonder why he was getting married. Now, as he drove, he searched very hard for a reason; his eyes darted around the street, took in the sycamore trees, the cherry blossom coming into pink, the road signs directing traffic to Manchester, but he could not find an answer. He loved Jeannie, most definitely he loved her, but she could be a bit of a wet weekend sometimes. And the thing with Terri was that she was fun. She was mouthy and bossy and always answered back, and he was sure she could be a royal pain in the arse when she wanted to be, but she probably never settled into one of those deep, sludgy silences the way that Jeannie did.

The truth was that night in Blackpool, the night he had proposed, he had been spurred on by a terrible remorse, a dark and clammy feeling that had wound its way around his legs and up to grip his belly, his chest, his brain. The previous weekend, several pints down at a shabby little nightclub named Legends on the edge of town, he had ended up in the club toilets with a girl whose name and face he could now no longer recall, though he remembered the dark roots of her hair and the scent of cheap toilet disinfectant, and how all the while he was screwing her he had stared at the same four words scratched into the cubicle wall: 'True Luv 4 Eva'.

In the days that followed he had felt sick and heavy with the knowledge of what he had done. He had bought Jeannie flowers, a bunch of yellow roses that she put in a vase by her bed and every time he had looked at them he winced. He had taken her to the pictures, complimented her dress, told her he loved her. None of it quelled the grey and filmy guilt swilling about in his belly like week-old dishwater. Eventually he decided the only thing that would make him feel better was to ask her to marry him.

There was nothing to be afraid of. He had been with

Jeannie for ever; she was a good girl, a little plain, a little pale, not the liveliest company, but they had grown up together, and he enjoyed the gentle tug of familiarity between them. And so his proposal was half an apology for a wrong she did not even know had been committed against her, and half a desire to be back in the time before he had strayed, where life was pure and simple and good, where there were no girls in short, tight dresses who tasted of Bacardi.

Now he wondered if he hadn't been rather rash. He was content enough, committed to the idea of a home and a family, but sometimes he wondered if he didn't feel just a bit too content. There were nights when it felt as if they had said everything they had to say to one another, and now their conversation dwelt only on topics that were in their eyeline: wedding plans, decorating, whatever was on the television.

Jimmy parked up along the road and sat for a moment while the engine cooled. He thought about Jeannie, her mousy hair on the pillow and her pile of clothes in the hall.

Rain pelleted the window, trickled down to the wiper and splayed. What would it be like, he wondered, to watch Terri undress? With the thought still warm in his mind, he opened the driver's door and climbed out into the wet morning. People were hurrying down the street in brisk, purposeful steps, and somewhere a car was coughing and spluttering to a damp start. He popped into the newsagent, bought cigarettes, a paper and a bottle of milk, made idle conversation with chubby Mr Hodge behind the counter, talked football, horses, weather.

He could smell the garage before he saw it: an intoxicating whiff of oil and petrol and paint. He loved that smell. 'Morning, lads!' Jimmy bellowed over the radio, which was rattling out chit-chat and jingles and traffic updates. 'Tea's up!' he called, and put the kettle on, fished out three teabags and found the mugs. 'Good morning, Angelica!' he cooed to the pin-up on the calendar above the sink. April. Two months till the wedding, he thought, before his eyes slid back up to the sweet-faced blonde in the red suspenders.

Bill and Dave came through then, talking about the Mini Metro in to be serviced, about its squeaky clutch and the respray on the bumper, and the Colt due in on Wednesday. 'On its last legs, that one,' said Bill. 'I said that to him last time. I said, you've got moss growing on your window-seals, lad, and I can fix that cheap enough but it's not a car to spend money on, this.' He shook his head. 'Did he listen? Did he 'eck. And now the gearbox is dicky ...' Bill was the owner of the garage. He was in his fifties, but his hair was still pitch-black, his shoulders were broad and his jaw square. He would have passed for an ageing matinée idol but for his legs, which were short and scrawny beneath his blue overalls. 'No matter what I did,' he once told the lads over a couple of ales, 'no matter what I ate, or how much I ran, I still had the legs of a pigeon.'

Now he washed his hands under the tap, lathering up the cheap green soap as he talked. 'It's the master cylinder on that Metro,' he said. 'We'll have to bleed a new one and ... Any biscuits?' he asked, and ferreted around in the old shortbread tin where they kept treats.

'You were looking pretty cosy with Terri on Saturday night!' Dave grinned at Jimmy. 'Something the missus should worry about?'

Jimmy turned his back on Angelica. 'Ehh,' he wiped a hand down his face. 'Not much of a memory on that one ...' he said sheepishly.

'A little the worse for wear, were we?' Dave laughed. 'So you won't recall sweet-talking her into taking you home for a nightcap?' Jimmy's face went pale, and Dave folded his arms. 'Fortunately,' he said, 'some of us were on hand to persuade you that this was not the behaviour of a soon-to-be-wedded man.'

'Fuck,' said Jimmy, and looked at his boots.

'Forget it.' Dave winked and picked up his tea. 'You're not the first man to get those last-minute pangs of desire, and no doubt you'll not be the last.'

'I think it was the booze talking,' Jimmy said.

'Did I ever tell you ...' Bill began.

'Probably,' said Dave, 'but go on ...'

'Cheeky bugger,' Bill laughed. 'Did I ever tell you about the beauty I met two days before I married Hazel?'

Hazel was Bill's wife, a thin, crotchety woman with short, fine hair and a face that suggested great and incomprehensible hardship. Whenever she bought biscuits for the garage they were always the dry, broken kind you could buy in discount bags at the market. She gave them own-brand teabags, and in all the years that Jimmy had worked for Bill he had never seen him eat a lunch of anything other than corned-beef sandwiches.

'Well, it was all booked, it was all arranged,' Bill said. 'And on the Thursday I went out for a drink with the lads, and in she swept, this vision, this beauty! Her name was Barbara, and the thing was she could barely speak English ...'

'Bill, how long have I worked for you?' Dave wondered. 'Eight years, is it? And how many times have you told me about the beautiful Barbara? Auburn curls and cherry-red lips ... I tell you what,' he shot a look at Jimmy, 'this Barbara is the only woman in the world who gets more beautiful with the years ...'

Bill laughed and went a little red. 'I don't regret it though, lads,' he said. 'For all her charms, I chose right, I chose my Hazel, and I married the best woman in the world.'

Jimmy and Dave looked at the floor, thinking of Hazel, with her thin mouth and her flat voice and her shapeless, sexless clothes. She made an unlikely subject for such devotion. Sometimes she would pop in to the garage, drop off toilet rolls and clean the kitchenette. 'Get rid of this filth,' she would mutter, and shove their pin-up calendar in the bin. Later they would have to fish it out again, and for much of January the object of their collective lust was tea-stained and smudged with instant coffee granules.

'Point is, lad,' Bill continued, 'your Jeannie is just like my Hazel. She's a keeper.' He patted Jimmy on the shoulder. Jimmy swallowed hard. He tried to imagine Jeannie thirty years down the line, but all he could picture was Hazel.

The day went fast enough. He enjoyed this routine: the teabreaks, the lunchtime butties, the steady straggle of phone-ins and golden oldies on the radio; he liked the banter and the satisfying process of mending something, the moment of sliding under the quiet, oily belly of a vehicle. Today, though, he was restless, anxious to be away from the chatter and the radio hits, and he was relieved when the afternoon light began to shift darker and the DJ announced the five o'clock news bulletin.

'All right, lads,' Bill huffed. 'Quick half?'

They sat in the Crown, and Jimmy toyed with his beer mat. Bill was at the bar. 'You all right, son?' Dave asked. 'You know I was just joking about that Terri stuff ... we've all been there.'

Jimmy tapped the mat against the table edge. 'Oh yeah, course, no harm done,' he said.

'And she's a good-looking lass, that Terri,' Dave added, 'you'd wouldn't be human if—'

'Oh yeah, yeah.' Jimmy nodded, and set the mat down as Bill returned with the round. 'And a bit of flirting never hurt anyone.'

The time seemed to drag that evening, Dave eager to discuss the pros and cons of a new motorbike, Bill wondering if the council ever planned to finish the road-works on Warrington Road. 'Because I tell you what, lads,' he said, 'I'm hard put to remember a time when there wasn't any works on that road. They had the water, then the gas … Next it'll be more of them ruddy mini roundabouts …'

When they left the pub the sky was lit up pink with long grey straggling clouds. Jimmy lifted his arm as he dashed across the road. 'See you in the morning, gentlemen!' he called, happy now they were parting, looking forward to being alone with his half-thoughts of Terri. He turned the ignition and sat for a moment. Jeannie would be home by now. He pictured her folded up on the sofa in a pair of black leggings and his old sweater, watching the local news. Maybe take the long route home, he thought, maybe stop off for a pint on his own.

The traffic was bad tonight, but he didn't particularly

mind. He rolled down the window and let in the sound of waiting cars, the steady growl, the faint huff of brakes. He breathed in the exhaust fumes and the scent of quickening spring, kept his eyes on the tail lights in front. After a few minutes he opened the glovebox and shuffled around until he found a cassette he liked, a little Oasis to put a stop to the DJ's mindless chatter. He turned it up loud to drown out the woman playing Pato Banton in the Golf in front.

As he rounded the corner there she was, sitting at the bus stop. She had on a short pink raincoat and black high-heeled boots and she was reading a magazine. He smiled and almost without thinking pulled in at the kerb. Terri looked up and squinted through the passenger door. 'Hop in?' Jimmy mouthed.

He remembered it later in slow-motion, the way she uncrossed her legs, stood up and shook her umbrella, the way she folded her magazine into her bag. It had that same fluid movement of the way she shucked gum, the way she did anything.

'I've waited half an hour for a bus!' she said as she climbed into the car. 'Every fifteen minutes they're meant to be!' She looked across at him. 'Thanks,' she said, and brushed her hand across his knee.

They spoke about the day behind them, and Jimmy found himself talking too long, too ramblingly about the Mini Metro and the way to bleed a gearbox, until he came to an awkward stop, coughed and asked Terri about her day.

He knew she worked in accounts for the council, in the sprawl of council offices near the town centre, and now she had unbuttoned the raincoat he could see her work clothes: a smart black skirt and a dark pink blouse that splayed a little over the bust. She was talking about her colleagues, about someone who was on a diet that involved only eating lemons or something. Jimmy was only half-listening, but he enjoyed the rise and fall of her voice, the fruity scent of her breath in this confined space.

He pulled up in the car park of the technical college. 'I'm sorry about Saturday,' he said, staring through the windscreen at some far, fixed point on the grey asphalt. 'I think I overstepped a mark.' The engine clicked and sighed as it settled, and from far above the lights of the night-school classrooms cast a warm orange glow. It felt strangely romantic.

'There's nothing to say sorry for,' Terri said. Her hand was back on his knee.

Jimmy lifted his arm from the steering wheel and traced his fingers along her face, down to the nape of her neck. In the quiet he heard the gentle yack-yack of her gum, felt her jawbone tense as she chewed.

'You'd better get going,' she said, so close he could feel her breath on his face. 'Your little wifey will be wondering where you are.'

They drove the rest of the way in near silence. Occasionally Terri would blurt out a direction. Left here. Right at the lights. This one, this one here. Her road was a short run of spruced-up terraces that led down to the railway embankment. He pulled over and she opened the door just a fraction. It was raining again now, and the gutters were full, rushing twigs and leaves and milk bottle tops towards the tracks.

'Thanks,' she said.

One hand on the door she turned back, stretched over and kissed his cheek. He turned his head a fraction too late, found his nose buried in the crease where her jaw and her ear and her neck all collided, where her skin smelled of gum and foundation and a dab of white musk.

And then she was gone, slamming the car door shut and reaching into her handbag for her house keys. He turned the car around and at the T-junction he paused, looked up to the rear-view mirror, watched her disappear through the front door.

A few minutes later Jimmy was still sitting at the junction, watching the traffic rushing through the early evening streets and the wipers sweeping the rain from left to right. He felt a little sick, as if he were driving too fast, too recklessly around a blind bend.

His hand found the gearstick, then the handbrake, and slowly he reversed back down the street, coming to a rest outside Terri's house. He looked up at her door, at the glossy green paint, and the shiny brass 26, at the primulas in the window boxes and the white nets in the window. He climbed out of the car and with a rising, giddy madness in his veins rang her doorbell.

She hadn't been surprised to see him. Jimmy sat in her lounge, now, contemplating the way she had smiled, her eyes knowing, half-amused, as she stood in the doorway. He imagined she had listened to him drive away, slipped off that pink raincoat of hers and, standing there in the hallway, between the telephone table and the coathooks, willed him to return. In truth, she had run upstairs, changed her knickers, made the bed and dabbed fresh scent where it mattered: the neck, the wrists, the inside of her thighs. She was powdering her face when the doorbell rang.

Terri's house was neat and crisp, with a cream sofa that faced the television, and a fireplace filled with a vase of dried poppy heads and decorative birch branches. He took in the collection of glass paperweights, the framed photographs of friends and family, the selection of women's magazines fanned out on the coffee table, and he was standing up, inspecting her CDs, when she returned to the lounge carrying two cans of lager.

She sat close to him on the sofa, her legs crossed so that one calf rested against his shin. 'Can I be honest with you, Jimmy?' she asked, and tapped one fingernail against her can. 'I have no idea why you're marrying that girl.' Jimmy ran his palms down to his knees. He didn't mind the physical side of things, he didn't mind sitting too close on another woman's sofa admiring the curve of her thigh, but he felt a little uneasy about actually saying something bad about Jeannie.

'It's complicated,' he began, then immediately frowned, because he couldn't think of how it was complicated at all. 'I mean, we've been together a long time, you know?' He looked up at her face, the pale blue eyes, the plump pink mouth, and what he wanted to say was 'I have no idea why I'm marrying that girl either. It was just a thing that got out of hand, a thing that took on a life of its own and now I have no idea how to stop it but I wish I could.'

But instead he took a long sip of his beer and then asked her why she didn't have a man. 'Have you seen any decent men in this town lately?' she laughed. 'Present company excepted, of course.'

She told him how she'd moved away after college, gone off to study hospitality and then dropped out. 'I was homesick and I couldn't see the point,' she explained. 'Me, sitting there in these student halls with my files all neat and my notebooks and my highlighter pens and all these textbooks, and I didn't have a fucking clue what I was doing.' She shrugged. 'I missed home, I missed my mum, and I didn't want to be a student, I fucking hate students. I wanted a job, so I could buy nice things and have a nice house and not live in some grotty student flat eating tinned spaghetti.'

Jimmy leaned back on the sofa. It felt very different to be with someone else. To sit in their home and talk about different things, different places, to argue about football and Arnold Schwarzenegger and whether you should have gravy on your chips. He thought of how he and Jeannie had shared so much of their lives, shared the same streets, the same schools, the same crowd, and now their conversation was like chewing the same piece of food, over and over, until it tasted of nothing. By the time he and Terri were halfway through their third beer, he had begun to feel content, to believe that this was a scenario that could work out very nicely. He slid his hand up her skirt.

Up in her bedroom Terri drew the curtains, switched on the bedside light, then sat on the end of the bed and took off her boots. Her air was more matter-of-fact than seductive, and Jimmy was surprised to see that she had been wearing a pair of tired pink ankle socks. He felt a little out of his depth now, but the beer was still warm in his veins, and the memory of kissing her, all lips and tongues and the taste of beer and fruit-flavoured gum, choked his doubts.

He glanced at the room: a floral duvet cover, a framed poster for the Moulin Rouge, a white bear holding a rose. The socks still distracted him. He crouched down on the carpet and picked up her first her left foot, then her right, cradled each heel in his palms and kissed her knee, then slowly peeled off the sock. Her toenails were painted bright red, and sat prettily against the beige carpet. He stopped and admired his handiwork. That was better, he thought.

But now he was down here he couldn't think how to get back on to the bed. It was awkward, he realised, canoodling with someone new. He picked up her foot again and kissed it.

'No one's ever kissed my feet before!' she giggled.

Did people kiss feet? Was he making a fool of himself? From somewhere in the depths of Jimmy's mind rose the half-memory of an article on seduction he had once read in a women's magazine. Trying to recall its directions, he slid his mouth around her big toe. It tasted of shoe leather and sweat and body lotion, not altogether repulsive, but not entirely erotic. He ran his tongue along the sole of her foot, feeling decidedly rueful that now, in the interests of fairness, he would have to do the other foot too. Still, it seemed to be having the desired effect. 'Where did you learn that?' she asked, and lay back on the bed.

It was all over fairly quickly, though for a while Jimmy successfully distracted himself by running a mental inventory of the parts of a Ford Cortina engine, and then wondering again about Jeannie's clothes piled in the hall.

Afterwards, Terri kissed his shoulders and ruffled his hair and went and put the kettle on while he stared at her sad pink ankle socks crumpled on the floor.

It was long dark when he left, slipping out of her front door and into the cool night air while Terri stood at the upstairs window, peeking through the curtains in her dressing-gown. Jimmy looked up and smiled before climbing into his car, pulled the driver's door firmly shut and settled down into his seat. In the semi-darkness he looked at the dashboard. A 1994 Vauxhall Corsa. Speedometer. Oil light. Ignition. He turned the key, and all the lights lit up. Life, he thought, in the old machine.

CHAPTER NINE

Since Wednesday it had been suddenly and unendurably hot. The town had wilted, cramming plump limbs into holiday clothes and emerging from their homes looking pale and dazed, skin pinkening, fringes sticking to foreheads and dark curves of sweat fanning under shirt sleeves. Defeated by the warmth, nobody seemed to do anything. They ate ice creams, pumped up paddling pools, and sat there in a few inches of cool water while the grass yellowed beneath them.

In the corner shops, children delved for ice pops in the freezer cabinets, women bought tall bottles of lemonade, lettuce, salad onions, boiled ham. 'It's too hot to eat,' they moaned, standing at the till, fanning themselves with their shopping lists. At night they lay awake, shifting and turning on damp sheets, listening to the sound of babies squalling across the street, to couples bickering late into the night.

People drove out to the coast, their bare legs clinging to the car upholstery, the steering wheel blistering under their palms. In the classrooms the windows were flung open, chalk dust stuck to dry lips, and the children wriggled their necks in their shirt collars as they copied out notes on coagulation, vectors, the subjunctive. Their pens slid in their fingertips and the pages of their exercise books dimpled under their clammy palms; even the ink seemed to run sticky and slow in this heat.

Outside, the air was heavy with corn flies, tiny black specks that stuck to faces and arms, that found their way into the folds of socks. They clung to windows and squeezed behind television screens. Years later they would still be found under the glass of picture frames, small dark motes on pale cream borders, a reminder of that brief, hot summer of 1994.

Jeannie spotted Danny sitting on the far side of the café, back against the wall, reading. On the table was a cup of tea and a tobacco tin. The bus station café was always busy, even on a hot Sunday morning, the room crowded with steam and fat and people who came and went, who shuffled up to the counter and ordered fried eggs and bacon barms, who sat stewing conversations over mugs of sweet tea.

'Hey,' she said, and he looked up to see her standing awkwardly by his table in a pair of denim shorts and a navy-blue vest, holding a can of orangeade. 'Reporting for duty,' she told him.

He noticed a slim orange crescent on her top lip and he smiled. 'Good work, soldier,' he said.

On Thursday afternoon Danny had appeared at the perfume counter, rested his freckled hands on the glass counter and called down to Jeannie, who was burrowing under the counter for extra bottles of fake tan.

'Hi!' She looked up, her face shiny and her hair flustered.

She had by now mastered some of the basic rules of good grooming, but the heat had undone her; by lunchtime each day she found the foundation had begun to slide off her face and shadow gathered in the creases of her eyelids. She powdered her forehead assiduously, but it had little effect.

'What are you doing Sunday?' Danny asked.

'Nothing,' she replied, smoothing her hair, running her thumbs over her eyelids.

'Good!' he smiled. 'Meet me at the bus station café, nine o'clock.'

She looked at him doubtfully. 'In the morning?'

He nodded.

'Where are we going?' she asked.

'Can't tell you.' He shook his head sorrowfully. 'Top secret information, I'm afraid.'

She laughed. 'All right, all right. Bus station café. Nine o'clock. I'll be the one wearing a pink carnation.'

His visit caused something of a stir among the other girls. 'Who's your friend?' called April.

'Oh ...' she blushed and looked at the counter-top, at the smudges where his fingertips had rested, 'no one.'

April looked at her. 'He's cute,' she said. 'Scruffy bugger, but cute.'

Jeannie shrugged and dipped back below the counter, feigning a return to the fake-tan hunt, but in truth she was trying to conceal the fluttering that had begun in her belly, spread up through her chest, and now fanned out on her face in a broad smile.

Jimmy was still asleep when she left that Sunday. He'd got home in the early hours; she'd heard him easing open the front door and padding lightly up the stairs, and now he didn't even stir as she rose, showered, dressed and placed a cup of tea for him by the bed. She knew it would be cold by the time he awoke, knew it would have grown filmy and grey, but she left it all the same, as a kind of apology for things she had done and the things she was about to do.

She walked into town. It was cooler at this hour, the morning air clearer and fresher and filled with bells. She passed the elderly couples making their way to church, the dog-walkers, the empty buses. She passed St Joseph's and heard the first settling notes of the organ and the choir rehearsing a hymn she remembered from school. She hummed the tune as she walked on along the streets until the words began to drift back into her head. 'Oh guide me, call me, draw me, / Uphold me to the end,' was as far as she remembered, but she repeated the words under her breath. It was, she recalled with a twinge of regret, about loyalty and devotion.

The centre of town was largely deserted. A handful of street cleaners on King Street swept up the rubble of Saturday night: the broken glass and vomit and kebab wrappers. A couple of girls still wearing last night's gaudy outfits walked barefoot along the pavement, arms linked, carrying their heels in their hands and laughing.

'I'm still drunk!' one cried, and their laughter rang through the empty town, bounced off the nightclub steps and the shuttered windows of the burger bar.

Jeannie looked up at the rooftops, at the sunlight hitting the shingles, and the church spire gleaming in the distance. The town looked prettier than she'd ever seen it.

She'd thought maybe they would be heading out to the countryside, to the quarry or Winter Hill or up to Rivington Pike, perhaps. It took a few moments for her to notice the two fishing-poles propped up behind Danny's seat.

'We're not going fishing?' she said.

'We are,' he replied, gathering together his bag and his book and picking up the poles. 'We're going fishing on the canal.'

The Sunday fishermen had been there for hours. They cast disgruntled looks at the new arrivals, the fair-weather fishers. They had foldaway seats and waterproofs, boxes and thermoses; they wore hats that kept the heat from their faces. Jeannie sat down in the grass by the canal's edge. The water was dark and dappled as a trout's back, stippled with sunlight and leaves.

Danny was setting out their equipment: two poles, line, hooks, pole rigs, plummets, a net ... 'Where did you get all this?' she asked, amused.

'My grandad,' he replied, reaching into the bag once again and bringing out a bottle of lemonade and a small bag of mints. 'Those are for us,' he added.

The heat was rising now, she could feel it on her neck, spreading up the backs of her arms. She leaned back in the grass and closed her eyes, enjoying the sun on her face, the rich, warm smell of the trees.

'So what do we do next?' she asked.

He brushed the hair from her forehead. 'Now we catch us some fish,' he said.

She kept her eyes closed, and his hand stayed cupping her face. 'What kind of fish?' She could hear him breathing, smell the tea on his breath.

'Tuna!' he said. 'Fishes as big as a man! Yellowfins!

Six feet long! Longer! They'll pull you in unless you're careful!'

She sprung her eyes open. 'Not really tuna though? In the Leeds–Liverpool canal?' She studied his face.

Danny bent down and kissed her lightly on the nose. 'No,' he whispered, 'no, most likely we'll catch some carp.'

She sat up and surveyed the row of houses across the canal. A family spilled out of one of the front doors and into a car carrying buckets and spades and a coolbox. The children were squealing on the back seat, and as they drove off one of them waved over to her from the open window.

He opened the tobacco tin and held it out towards her. It squirmed with maggots, pale bodies twitching and writhing in the sudden brightness. 'Bait,' he announced.

Jeannie shuddered. 'Oh God,' she said tightly, 'I fucking hate maggots.'

Danny pushed a fingertip into the tin. 'There's nothing to be scared of,' he told her. 'They're just little things, they're not going to hurt you.' Jeannie shuffled uneasily in the grass.

'Here,' he said, 'let me show you. This is what you do on cold mornings, when you've got to keep your bait warm …'

He picked a single maggot from the tin and placed it

under his tongue. Jeannie squealed. The other fishermen looked over and scowled. She clamped her hands over her mouth.

'Oh my God,' she whispered, eyes wide. 'Oh my God, I am never kissing you again!'

Danny began to laugh. He spat the maggot into his palm and tipped it back into the tin where it melded back into the crowd. 'Your turn,' he told Jeannie. She shook her head violently. 'Jeannie, come on! Live a little!' he said, picking out another specimen with his finger and thumb.

'It's a maggot!' she hissed.

'I know!' he smirked. 'A tiny little maggot! It's not going to bite you! Come on, open wide …'

She looked him straight in the eye and slowly opened her mouth.

'Lift your tongue,' he told her. 'Good girl.' He dropped the maggot into her mouth, covered her lips with his hand.

A look of quiet terror spread across her face. He stared at her, surely, steadily, a little ruthlessly, as if breaking an unruly horse. Jeannie slackened her jaw, felt the maggot dancing beneath her tongue. Twisting and turning and wriggling. It was nothing more than popping candy, she told herself; she could do this, she could do this. She breathed through her nose, looked up at Danny. He held her gaze, ten seconds, twenty, then cupped her face in his hands and kissed her lips.

'Spit,' he instructed, and the maggot landed in his palm in a pool of orangeade spittle.

'So you've got to feed them bait first,' he told her, picking out some of the maggots, maybe six or seven, and flinging them into the water. They speckled the surface then disappeared. Jeannie stared at the spot where the maggots had vanished, ran her tongue across her teeth.

'What happens now?' she whispered. He kept his eyes on the canal for a moment, then picked out a few more of the maggots.

'You keep feeding them,' he answered quietly, without looking at her.

She felt as if she were back in double chemistry, scoring the answers from someone who had been paying attention instead of staring blankly out of the classroom window. She slipped her fingers into the tobacco tin, lifted four fat maggots and scattered them into the water.

He showed her how to attach the float, how to hook the bait and plumb the depths. Then they sat, and they waited. The day was full-blown now, the towpath milling with cyclists, and families coerced into Sunday promenades. Once in a while a barge came by, slicing through the reflection of the heavy blue sky, stirring the surface so the weeds and the leaf-litter swirled and the great smooth ripples spread wider and wider until they rocked up against the banks.

The barges were painted with roses and diamonds and

castles, lacquered in thick red and blue and bottle-green, with their names scrolled on the side: *Catweasel*, *Drummer Boy*, *Maria*.

'Good morning!' called the people on board, standing at the stern. 'Hello there!' they hollered, waving and smiling as their boats floated slowly, softly by.

'It makes me want to go for a swim,' Jeannie said when the water was smooth again.

'I wouldn't,' Danny told her. 'Every summer people go swimming and drown in the canal.' He was quiet for a moment. 'I saw a man drowned once,' he said sharply. 'A hot day, like this, middle of summer. They said he'd been drinking, smoking weed, said he wasn't all right in the head. He'd walked miles across the fields to get there, walked straight, right through the field, through the crops, as the crow flies.'

Jeannie pictured two strong legs swishing through the oat fields, arms swinging at his sides, fingers grazing the grain. She pictured the plump, green kernels of the oats, the balmy smell they gave off on warm days and the long frondy whiskers that tickled your skin.

'There were these two women riding their horses who saw him,' Danny continued, 'they said he just came up out of the fields and ran down to the canal and jumped. And I guess he must have been drunk or stoned, or got himself caught on something, because he didn't come up again, not for a long time.'

She pictured the field thinning out, the gold giving way to green as he neared the banks of the canal. She imagined the soil grown dry and dusty in the heat, the man's feet hot and swollen in his shoes, and his head aflame with cheap liquor, she pictured his unquenchable thirst.

'When I got there they were hauling him out,' Danny said. 'The women were holding their horses and crying, and the ambulance men had a stretcher ready, and there was a policeman taking statements. And I just remember his face, the way his head rolled back and his eyes were all glassy and his mouth wide open. They laid him out on the towpath and cleared his tongue and pumped his chest and all that, but it was too late. He was just lying there, his hair drying in the sun, and his T-shirt clinging to his belly.'

Jeannie looked at the canal, still and sweet and placid in the lunchtime sun. Above their heads hung the pale underside of the alder leaves, and from somewhere nearby they could hear a moorhen currucking and the soft pitt-pitting of a coot. It seemed impossible that anyone could drown in a place like this.

'Who was he?' she asked.

'His name was Steven Jones, he came from Ince, and he was thirty-two. I read about him in the paper,' Danny said. 'I got sort of obsessed with drowning after that. I was fifteen and maybe a bit macabre. I used to go to the library and read all the books about local murders – you know, men who poisoned their wives with arsenic and all that. But after this I only wanted to read about drowning, I wanted to know how it happens and how it would feel.'

'And?' Jeannie asked.

'It's slower than you think. Once your face goes under the water your heart slows down, and the blood stops flowing around your body. Your blood shifts, that's what they call it, blood shift, up to here,' he tapped his chest, 'to stop your lungs collapsing under the weight of the water. And if you're conscious, like he must've been, you'll try to hold your breath, try to find some air, and you'll panic and thrash about a bit, which all the while is using more oxygen. And then eventually you'll breathe in. Your body can't help it, it'll just inhale. And then you're breathing in water. It doesn't go to your lungs though, not right away; instead all that dirty canal water would've gone into his stomach. It's only later it fills your lungs, and then you're drowned.'

She floated a blade of grass on to the water. 'That's a horrible way to die,' she said.

'Maybe, maybe not,' he said. 'I mean you panic, right, but then you're unconscious. You don't even know you're drowning. He wouldn't have known, not really. It was a hot day and he walked all that way through the fields, and all he wanted was to cool off in the canal. I kept thinking how good that water must've felt when he first jumped in.'

They didn't say anything for a while after that. They looked at the fishing-lines in the water and the reeds that had grown tall now, hiding the warbler nests, and at the clouds of midges that flitted and jigged in the air.

'Look at this!' There came a shout from along the bank. They looked up and saw a boy of about eight, bare-chested in a pair of tracksuit bottoms and carrying a short orange fishing-rod. He had leaped up on the bank where he had been throwing pieces of bread, and was now pointing at a patch of the canal by the bridge, hopping from one foot to the other with excitement. They stared at him for a moment, dancing about on the grass.

'Mind this,' Jeannie said to Danny, handing him her pole, then she walked over to where the boy was pointing. Below the bank a shoal of small slim fish tickled the surface, pale shapes in the dark water. She pictured Steven Jones's fingers, cold and still beneath the waterlip. This was the thing about the canal: it had secrets.

'What are they?' she asked the boy. She could smell his clammy skin in the heat: a clean, sweet, childish scent.

'Dunno.' He gave an exaggerated shrug. 'Tiddlers,' he said, and he followed them as they swam further up the canal. 'I'm going to the ponds!' he called back to her. 'Tons of fish there. They're jumping out of the water!'

He waved his arms about as if portraying an explosion of fish. Jeannie smiled and waved.

She sank back on to the bank beside Danny. 'Maybe we should go to the pond,' she sighed. 'We've been here four hours and we've not caught a thing.'

Danny smiled. 'Patience,' he told her. 'Good things come to those who wait.'

She clucked her tongue. 'And I'm hungry,' she told him. 'I didn't have any breakfast.'

'All right, all right,' he laughed. 'Half an hour more, and then we'll go and find you some food. Deal?'

'Deal,' she said, and bending over the canal edge, she addressed the water: 'Did you hear that, fishes? You've got half an hour to bite.'

It was the hottest it had been all week. All across the town people were lighting barbecues and putting out garden furniture and getting a little afternoon drunk with the neighbours. Jeannie wondered what Jimmy had done with his day. Perhaps he was still in bed, perhaps he was spreadeagled on the patio basking in his Sunday hangover.

She saw the lily pads sway. 'Look!' she breathed and pointed at the water. The water-lilies had bloomed a little early this year, their fat yellow flowers spreading in the sunlight, and now their broad leaves were shifting and shuffling as something moved in the shadows beneath.

'OK, OK,' Danny said quietly. 'Stay very, very, still ... We've got something! We've got something! It's bitten! Quick!'

He shoved the fishing-pole into Jeannie's hands, and she felt the weight of the fish on the line.

'What do I do?' she asked, her arms frozen, her eyes full of panic.

'Reel it in!' he said.

The fish swung out of the water, twisting and flipping on the hook. Drops of water scattered through the blue and the afternoon sunlight hit its scales. It was a beautiful thing to behold.

'It's a chub!' Danny cried. 'We've caught a chub!'

On the bank he knelt down and took the fish in his hands. The hook was caught in its lip. Jeannie crouched in the grass and watched. The chub stared up, opened and shut its mouth, fluttered its tail.

With one hand Danny gripped it below the gills and with the other reached into its mouth and gently dislodged the hook, eased it out the same way it had come.

'Here,' he said to Jeannie,' you should hold it.' She shook her head, held her hands behind her back. 'It's your catch!' He stretched his arms out towards her. 'Hold it!'

She took the chub, softly, delicately, reluctantly. It felt smooth and heavy in her hands. Its scales ran a mottled silver along its back, and its face was a translucent pink, lips curving downwards in a pale pinkish-grey, and its eye staring up, round and golden and bewildered.

'What do we do with it?' she asked.

'Well you can keep it and eat it, or you can throw it back,' he said, watching her face.

She looked at the fish, gasping in the heat, and her lungs felt tight. Its pale mouth gaped open and shut, over and over, as if fighting to speak.

She thought again of Steven Jones, hot, red-faced from the fields, leaping into the canal on a day like today, of his lungs filling with water, of him lying dead on the bank in the warm afternoon sunshine. She cradled the chub, felt it twitch and pulse as she bent over the long grass and slipped it back into the dark canal water.

She was quiet as they walked back along the towpath. Her right shoe rubbed her heel and distracted her from thoughts of the fish and the drowning man. They passed Top Lock and the old coal and iron works, where mounds of rubble and earth could be seen beyond the trees. A little further on they stopped where a couple of pleasure-boaters were making their way through the lock; they had sailed their barge through the gates and into the chamber, and now they were working the sluice gate open, so they could sail on up the flight. It was a slow, laborious method of escape. Jeannie and Danny stood on the bank and watched the water rise, slowly edging up the smooth dark stone, where the weeds clung green and bright in the crevices.

'Isn't this weather glorious?' called the man working the lock. He had on just a pair of white shorts, and his shoulders and his chest and his nose and his bald head shone red with sunburn, as his wife squatted nearby, pale and toadish beneath a broad-brimmed hat. Jeannie nodded, but his joviality seemed misplaced now, as if the day had darkened and soured.

They walked on in silence, listening to the shuffle of the fishing gear in the bag he carried, the rattle of the poles, the soft give of the ground beneath their feet. They came to a halt by a green metal sign that pointed up over the embankment.

'Let's go to the plantations,' Danny said, and started off through the long grass.

She hesitated, stood on the bank until he seemed to disappear, and all that was left was the thrashing sound of his steps and the top of the fishing-poles, bobbing above the green.

'Come on!' She heard his voice muffled by grass and warm air, and she smiled and waded in behind him.

The plantations stretched across acres, wide green fields that ran south-westward and at this time of year stood tall and strong and deepest green. The soil around here was rich with clay and lay upon shale rock, and so they grew wheat and oats and potatoes. After the rabble of the town, after the close-set terraces and the clutter of the factories and the estates, the plantations were a still green pool, quiet and smooth as a millpond. At one time, out of these fields rose the black metal spines of pit shafts, the area having once been famed for its cannel coal, which burned brightly and fiercely and left little of itself behind. The seam had run dry now, though the ground was still threaded with soughs, the old drainage tunnels that now fed minewater into the streams, iron-rich and ochred, colouring the plants and discouraging the fish, letting the past seep into the present.

The plantations circled the Hall, a handsome, grey-stone building where they held weddings and craft fairs, where there were tea rooms, walled gardens, playgrounds and a miniature railway. Today it would be heaving with families, people filling the car parks and the walkways, teeming around the lily ponds and the nature trails, swarms of children descending upon the swings and the climbing frames. It seemed that on hot days the people appeared here the way ants spilled out from the cracks in the paving stones, suddenly and in vast numbers, all charging in the same direction as if compelled by some great, irresistible force.

Nearby, in the village, it was quiet, a stone church that looked down over the fields, a pub that sat open yet empty, a lane that ran cool and dark beneath the shade of the trees. It felt undisturbed, disused, a front room, kept for best. She was watching their feet crossing patches of sunlight and shadow and listening to Danny's voice telling her about Miles Davis. In truth, Danny had never really listened to Miles Davis. He owned a copy of *Kind of Blue*, certainly – a copy that was dog-eared and scratched and twenty pence from the charity shop, and that he had held many times, pressed its cardboard sleeve into his palms, read the words on its flipside, looked at the picture of a black man in suit and tie, eyes dipped, lips pressed up against the mouth of a trumpet, as if he were sipping at it. But he had never actually listened to it. *Kind of Blue* was really just another of Danny's affectations, an accessory he carried, like his Allen Ginsberg poems and the pouches of loose tobacco he liked to buy.

The heat had got to him a little now, aroused a restlessness that made his skin prickle. He had a desire to do something, to make something happen. He kicked out at a small grey pebble on the road, sent it skidding across the tarmac, but Jeannie carried on walking, silent and unprovoked. He felt frustrated by her suddenly, by her plainness and her quietness, by her lack of ambition. At this moment she appeared no different to everyone else around here, and yet never had it seemed more important that she was different, that she wasn't just a meek little girl who sold perfume, that like him she didn't belong in this town, she was something more, something braver.

'The problem with this place,' he waved an arm towards the town, lying peaceful and sun-soaked in the distance, 'is that all these people aren't living. They're just stagnating. They've never acted on their own thoughts, they've just followed the same thoughts as everyone else, the same thoughts as their neighbours next door, and the same thoughts their parents had, and their parents before them.' He was riled up now and it felt good, talking with his fists clenched and the taste of bile on his tongue. 'So you get a job, so you can earn some money, right?' he ploughed on. 'And what do you use that money for? You use it to buy a house. And then you've got your house and you've got your mortgage, and you use your money to get a better car because that's what you're supposed to do, or you use it to buy dresses and microwaves and timeshares. And no one questions it, no one says "Is this what I want? Do I want to spend my life married to this woman and mowing the lawn and saving up for a new sofa and going to the carvery on a Sunday?"' He looked at Jeannie, his eyes triumphant. 'No one asks those questions because they're all terrified. They're all crouching in their perfect little houses scared the roof is going to fall in because they don't have the right handbag or the right bathroom suite or they've run out of kitchen roll.'

He stopped, and the lane fell quiet again. He had

perhaps gone a little further than he intended, he thought, and glanced apologetically at the houses in the distance. He was, after all, rather fond of the gentle rhythms of this town, with the way that it remained so rooted in routine, Sunday roast and Friday fish and Wednesday's half-day closing. It was considered and ingrained and wanted bravery and impulse; it wasn't as if it were without its own metre, its own music. He looked over at Jeannie, at the light through the leaves dappling her face and her shoulders. The vest was old and fitted snugly, and her shorts had obviously once been a pair of jeans, hacked off unevenly with a pair of kitchen scissors. Beneath them, her legs were pale and unused to the air, carrying the blueish-grey sheen of skimmed milk. He felt fond of her again now, now that his anger had loosened and cooled and he reached out a hand and ruffled her hair.

She smoothed it back into place and folded her arms across her chest as they walked. Sometimes it was thrilling to hear him talk this way, to let it stir you up and carry you along. There were moments when she wished she could feel his excitement about Miles Davis records, or all these crazy poems he showed her, or the idea of going somewhere with no money and no plan. But more often she recoiled a little, wrinkled her nose as if all this wild-eyed talk carried a stench like milk on the turn. There was something suspect about it, something doubtful; when he talked like this she found it hard to believe him.

She was doubting everything lately; not just whether or not she wanted to marry Jimmy, or whether she wanted to stay here and sell bottles of perfume and jars of face cream for ever, but also her feelings for Danny, for someone she realised she barely knew at all.

The doubts followed her everywhere. They stared back at her as she fixed her lipstick in the bathroom mirror, and they were there in the whistle of the kettle and the squeal of the bus tyres and the hiss of the perfume bottle; at night as she tried to sleep they circled her head, like the seagulls cawing and diving and screeching above the rubbish tip on the edge of town. But there were times too, like now, that she only had to look at him, at his freckled arms, at his strong blue eyes, and her heart leapt and her blood rushed, and she felt her faith restored.

They had walked along the lane and were halfway back across the fields when the weather broke. There had been a sense of rising dust, a closeness and a thickening, as if the day was curdling. The sky seemed to groan and creak, and then the rain fell with the plump, heavy certainty of perfectly ripe fruit.

'Shit!' she said, and looked about for cover.

'A little water won't hurt you!' he smiled, standing stock-still in the wheat.

'Right, yeah,' she laughed at him, already sopping, the rain flattening his hair. 'I think we've had enough drownings for one day.'

It rained all the way home; rain that fell blindly, that blackened the sky and crashed through the fields, bending the crops and flooding the streams. They took off their shoes and took off their socks and walked barefoot through the wet, and the tall grass prickled their ankles and the black silt caught between their toes, and as they walked they sang – primary school hymns, show tunes and soul standards, songs about God and girls, about love and lust.

Outside his grandad's front door he paused. 'Cup of tea?' he offered, and looked down at her, standing drenched and dishevelled on the pavement, barefoot with a fishing-pole in her hand. 'I'll take that as a yes,' he said.

It was quiet in the hallway. 'Hello?' he called through the house, but there was no reply. 'He's such a dirty stop-out, my grandad,' he told her. 'Now stay there a minute,' he said, and went tiptoeing over the carpet while she stood dripping on the mat. It seemed a nice house, old-fashioned and well-polished. There was a mirror hanging above the phone table and she caught sight of herself, hair dark and wet and clinging to her neck in long seaweedy fronds, her make-up long gone, and her vest soaked right through.

Danny reappeared carrying a copy of the *Evening Post*, peeling off a page for every step he took along the hall and placing it on the carpet. 'There!' he said, triumphantly. 'Kettle's on. I'll run the bath.'

And off he went, slowly climbing the stairs, while Jeannie followed the path of newspaper into the lounge, her footsteps dampening the stories of local robberies and beauty queens, a fundraising hike and a church picnic, adverts for cut-price tiles and the largest fireplace show-room in the North-West.

She couldn't sit down, of course, and so instead she stood there in the middle of the lounge, listening to the rattle and squeak of the bath taps, the jovial chug and splutter of the water making its way up through the pipes. The room was small but neat, and seemingly little-changed since the 1950s: its walls papered glossy cream and the carpet running a geometric pattern of green and cream and rust. There was a yellow felt tablecloth and matching curtains, and a small sofa and two easy chairs in a slubby bottle-green. High up above her head a wooden laundry rack was suspended on a pulley system, and by the door she noticed a bookcase crammed with old copies of *Reader's Digest*.

Most of the ornaments were holiday souvenirs: on the dresser, a framed black and white photograph of Margate,

a Cornish piskie, bears from Canada, stags from Scotland,
buffalo from America and several Welsh lace doilies settling
pieces of blue Wedgwood pottery: a cup, a vase, a sugar
bowl. There were commemorative china cups in the
cabinet, a plate on the wall that marked 1978 and showed
the complete Chinese zodiac, and a cuckoo clock from
a week in Switzerland, that no longer marked the hour
but still kept the time with a constant broodish cluck.

On the chimneybreast hung letter-openers, corkscrews,
and below them on the mantelpiece ran a selection of
brass trinkets: ducks and deer, elephants and owls and
little ladies in bonnets and broad skirts that, when lifted,
revealed themselves to be tiny bells. Propped among them
was a postcard. She picked it up between damp finger
and thumb and looked at the picture, a scene of ponies
and gorse in blue-skied Exmoor. She flipped it over and
squinted at the handwriting, old-fashioned and left-
slanted in spidery blue ink, a message that said everything and nothing: 'Having a lovely time these few days.
Weather glorious. Hotel fine. Off to Dunster Castle
tomorrow. Hope this finds you well. Fondest love,
Margaret.' She propped it back against the lamp and stood,
and dripped, and waited for Danny to return.

He seemed to undress almost without thinking. She was
standing by the bathroom door and looked up from her
feet to find him naked. You could see quite clearly the

line of his T-shirt, the boundaries on his arms and his chest that divided sun-pinkened freckles from bright white skin. On his legs, the freckles climbed to mid-thigh then stopped abruptly, some remnant, presumably, of a short-wearing youth. She kept her eyes trained chastely on the freckled areas, and fiddled with her fingernails, delaying the moment when she too would have to undress. 'Come on,' he said quietly, 'don't be shy.'

She could count on one hand the number of men who had ever seen her naked. She looked at the window, at the rain still hammering against the glass, and held the hem of her vest quite tightly before peeling it over her head. He sat down on the edge of the bath, the smooth, cool porcelain pressing against his bare flesh, and watched her standing in the middle of the room with eyes closed, as she fiddled with the button on her shorts. Without her clothes, she looked even paler and quieter, like a rabbit skinned, a pheasant plucked. He took in the jut of her ribs and her hips, and the hard wishbone of her chest. She was all sharp and awkward, save for the small, smooth curve of her belly.

She opened her eyes to find him looking at her and so she stared at the bathmat and said stiffly, 'The water'll get cold …' and he smiled and held out his hand to help her into the tub.

She sat in the smooth end and scrunched up her legs and wrapped her arms around her knees.

'I haven't shared a bath with anyone since I was a kid,' she said as he climbed in and rested his back against the taps.

'Seems baths may have shrunk a bit since then,' he laughed and shuffled his legs about. 'Tell you what, tell you what,' he said, 'budge up, and I'll sit behind you … right … there we go, that's better.'

It was not the most graceful of manoeuvres, the water pitching up and over the side of the bath as he stood, and again as he sat down, but it was certainly a more comfortable arrangement than before and meant that they were spared the embarrassment of looking at each other naked in the water.

'See, this is better,' he told her. 'How else was I supposed to scrub your back?'

It was peaceful listening to the rain, and the lap of the water against the bathtub, and the gentle snappling sound as he lathered a bar of green Lux soap between his palms.

'So tell me about growing up and sharing baths,' he said.

'Well,' she began, and then bit her lip as his hands touched her shoulder-blades, ran down her back, across her spine and up again. 'It was me and my sister,' she said. 'Sunday night was bath night. We did everything together then. Our mum even used to dress us the same, little ra-ra skirts and buckle shoes and white ankle socks. But even so, we were always different.'

'How so?' he asked.

'Well, when we were out playing, she'd be cartwheeling and handstanding and flashing her knickers, she knew all the skipping rhymes and the clapping songs. She could rollerskate and hula-hoop and disco dance and everybody loved her.'

He scooped a jug-load of bathwater over her hair as she talked, watched it turn from fine and mousy to something glossier, darker. Warm soapy water trickled down her forehead.

'I mean, I loved her too,' she added, in case he mistook anything for jealousy. He squeezed the shampoo out of the bottle, amber-coloured and the faintest scent of alpine herbs.

'And what about you?' he asked. 'What were you doing when she was skipping and rollerskating and making everyone fall in love with her?' He liked the feel of her hair bundled beneath his hands, all warm and damp and soapy.

'Oh, I was … I don't know!' Jeannie laughed. 'I was probably rollerskating six feet behind her on the pavement, praying I didn't fall over.'

Danny laughed and kneaded her hair.

'To be honest, I've always been just average at everything. I wasn't daft at school, but I wasn't so smart either. I wasn't pretty and I wasn't funny and I wasn't especially good at sports. You asked me once why I'm working selling perfume in a department store, and that's your answer: it's because I'm average, and I'm doing an average job in an average town.'

He sank the plastic jug beneath the water again. 'But you don't have to be average,' he told her. 'You could do anything, and you could go anywhere and be anyone. You could even learn how to cartwheel if you wanted to.' He poured the water over her hair, watched the foam slip down her back.

'I don't know,' she replied. 'I'm not sad about it exactly … I mean, I've got along just fine without handstands. It's only sometimes when I just don't really have a clue what I'm good at and what I'm meant to do or where I'm meant to go, and I wonder if I'm just going to drift on like this for ever, waiting for things to happen to me.'

He swept the long wet strands of hair to the side, pressed his lips against her shoulder and breathed in the warm, soapy scent of her skin. 'Or maybe you could make things happen,' he said.

They sat like that for a long time, wrapped around one another until the water was cool and clouded with soap, until it clung to their skin in foamy grey lines.

He lifted his face from her shoulder. 'Come on,' he said, 'let's get dry.'

He heaved himself out of the bath and his feet spread broad puddles all across the cool lino. The towels were faded and soft, old man's bath-sheets that had begun to fray at the edges.

'I don't have any dry clothes,' she realised, standing in her bath-sheet, looking at the sad little heap of her shorts and her vest, sitting by the door.

'Ah,' he said. 'Yes, good point. Well, you could wear something of mine, maybe ... Oh, wait,' he said, beginning to smile. 'I know what we should do ...'

His grandfather's bedroom sat at the front of the house. It smelled warm and powdery and a little musty. Danny switched on the light. There was a kidney-shaped dressing-table still set out with his grandmother's belongings: a hairbrush, an ornate tissue box, a powder puff in a lidded cut-glass bowl that looked like a jellyfish. On a small metal tray there was a compact and a lipstick, and a perfume bottle with a yellow tassel about its neck. The bed covers had been tucked in tightly, a strip of sheet running at the top, crisp and white as royal icing. On a small cupboard stood a water glass, an alarm clock, a bedside light. It was a sad thing to see: a bed that had been only half-used for more than twenty years.

The wardrobe was a handsome dark mahogany, two-sided, and its deep bottom drawer adorned with brass handles. In the middle was a long mirror, and above it a floral pattern had been inlaid in the wood. Danny unlocked the left-hand door to reveal a row of women's clothes.

'My grandmother's,' he told her. 'Smell them.'

They pressed their faces into the dresses and the coats and the scent of age and grease and old perfume rose up to meet them. It was bewitching, the smell of another era, a time when fabrics were finer and fragrances heavier.

'Choose something,' he said, and she brushed her hand along the serge and the silk and the chiffon. There were blouses in mint-green silk and daffodil-yellow, long floral dresses, embroidered cardigans, fitted skirts and matching jackets in stern-coloured tweed.

'I feel a bit weird about it,' she said. 'You know, it's your grandmother's things ... Wouldn't your grandad be upset?'

Danny sat on the edge of the bed. 'No, no, you know, I think he'd be happy someone lovely was wearing them.'

She laughed lightly and gathered the bath-sheet tightly around her. 'OK,' she said. 'Well then, help me choose?'

He dressed her in a pale slip that gaped in the bust but clung to her hips, its neckline hemmed with a fine ruffle of lace and ribbon. And then a blue summer dress that gathered at the waist and zipped at the side and had short, pretty sleeves that puffed up and out. He looked at her standing before the wardrobe, her face still faintly flushed from the bath, her hair half-dry, and brushed back from her brow. She had, he decided, never looked prettier. He reached down a square lidded box from on top of the wardrobe, and took out a cherry-red hat, decorated with velvet flowers and a net that draped across the face.

'Here,' he said, and he placed the hat gently on her head and tucked her hair behind her ears. The red net brought out the grey of her eyes, the pink of her lips and the flush of her cheeks.

Danny opened the right-hand side of the wardrobe, where his grandad's clothes hung, more muted and mottled than his grandmother's selection. He took out a vest, and a cream shirt with a starched collar, and a tweedy brown suit with braces and a waistcoat. They fitted surprisingly well, and he smiled as he buttoned up the waistcoat.

'I could get used to this,' he said, smoothing his damp hair into a neat parting and pulling a greenish necktie from the rail on the wardrobe door. When he was finished and fixed he linked his arm through Jeannie's and they stood and looked at themselves in the mirror, standing barefoot in their finery.

'Don't we look dapper?' he said.

'You scrub up very nicely indeed, young man,' she told him, and shuffled his tie so it met the neck of his shirt. She remembered the last time she had looked at herself all dressed up, standing queasy and unhappy in the bridal shop fitting room, and she held her breath until the surge of guilt passed.

She picked up Danny's hand and planted a kiss in his

palm. 'Thank you,' she said, half to his hand, and half to him.

He smiled. 'Let's celebrate with a sherry!' he said, and led her out on to the landing and back down the stairs.

'Choose a record,' he told her as he set out two tumblers on the yellow felt table top, measured out three fingers of Bristol Cream and topped it up with tonic water. She hadn't noticed the record-player earlier, or the small clutch of vinyl sitting together on a chair behind the green sofa.

She flicked through the records, John Coltrane, David Bowie, Peggy Lee, Joan Baez, Ray Charles, Benny Goodman … None of them were new, and some still carried their charity shop price stickers: 30p from the Sue Ryder, 15p from Marie Curie, 40p from the Hospice. She held up a Bob Dylan record.

'This one,' she told him, and hoped he might be impressed.

'Ah, a bit of Bobby Dylan, eh?' he said, handing over her glass of sherry. 'Good choice.'

She took a slug of her drink while he slipped the record from its sleeve. The sherry tasted thin and dry, it clung to her teeth and then rushed against her tongue. She thought she might quite like it. Danny crouched over the turntable, the record poised gently between his fingertips, and lowered it on to the spindle. There was a low, rhythmic, rolling sound as the vinyl revolved, like a train far, far, away in the distance, and then came a faint crackle and fizz as the stylus kissed the groove.

Jeannie had drunk most of her sherry and tonic by the time he straightened up and turned round. Danny laughed at the empty glass.

'Top-up?' he asked, and she nodded as the music began to play.

It rose up out of the record-player speakers, guitar, Hammond, harmonica meeting with the soft roar of the rain; it filled the room, touched the height of the laundry-rack, found its way into the folds of her dress, stories of red-headed women and walks along old canals, Italian poets and topless bars and corkscrews to the heart.

They drank their sherry, and he took her hand, drew her in close, the way he'd seen men do in old Sunday afternoon films. Then around they went, dancing across the room, spinning over the giddy carpet, all around the green sofa and the easy chairs and the yellow-felted table, while the cuckoo clock clucked and bell-skirted brass ladies looked on, and the sherry sank lower in the bottle.

CHAPTER TEN

Danny boarded the number 17 at the bus stop on the corner. The town was bright and clear this morning, washed clean by last night's thunderstorm, the windows shone quite ferociously, the dust had lifted from the pavements, and the birds were singing madly, thrilled by the fresh, wet soil all a-wriggle with insects.

He sat down opposite a blonde woman reading a magazine, sized up her summer frock, her sturdy calves, her proud, plump cleavage. Not his sort, he concluded, though there was something a little compelling about this sort of woman, the type for whom the word 'broad' must surely have been coined.

Terri could feel the man's eyes on her. She was used to being admired. Courted it, even. And now to while away the journey and bring a spark to the morning she ruffled her feathers a little: dipped her magazine to allow him a better view of her bosom, parted her lips, uncrossed then recrossed her legs.

He knew what she was up to, and he toyed with the idea of flirting with her, but this morning his thoughts were full of Jeannie in his grandmother's hat, his hand on her back, the brush of the carpet beneath their feet.

When she had left last night they had kissed in the hallway, he had stood, one hand on the Yale lock, his body pressing her against the wall. Could he have slept with her? Probably, he decided. But he was concerned that sex with Jeannie might rather sully the picture he had painted of them, which, now he thought about it, was rather pure and rather wholesome.

The sight of her naked body yesterday had not proved erotic so much as reassuring. When they did sleep together it would be far away from here, far away from these streets and this rain, a boarding house on the south coast maybe.

This was the idea that had begun to shape in his mind this morning: he was going to ask her to run away with him, to catch the southbound train, to leave their stupid jobs, leave everything behind and just go.

Should she up her game? Terri was perturbed that the man in the opposite seat had barely registered her little display, and instead seemed to be staring out of the window at the passing houses. It was a game of chess, she told herself, and all she had to do was think of her next move. She was quite certain she could win this.

There was a gleam of triumph to Terri today; Jimmy had been over nearly every night since their first encounter, and yesterday he had even skipped football to see her, sitting out in the back garden, bare-chested in his shorts while she sunned herself in her red bikini.

On Saturday night she had cooked him dinner – fillet steak and chips, then chocolate ice cream, no bowls, one spoon, for afters. She'd fetched a bottle of white wine, lit some candles and worn the little black satiny dress she'd bought for last year's Christmas work do. Terri relished the routine of seduction, enjoyed the ABC of it, the long-rehearsed dance of wooing a man. She liked, too, all the paraphernalia of romance: the roses and the teddy bears, the lingerie and the nicknames, the things that she could proudly wear, as if to say 'there is a man who loves me'.

She had never been the prettiest girl in her class, but she was certainly the most accommodating – even she was surprised when she scraped through her GCSEs, since as far as she, or anyone else, could seem to remember she had spent the six-week stretch of her study leave bestowing hand-jobs on sixth-form boys.

Now she was older, she had grown more subtle in her art, had learned the power of a certain glance or a tilt of the chin, had begun to appreciate the idea that being desired is often more entertaining than being available. She took little satisfaction from her job, from the endless routine of paper-pushing, filing cabinets and office management, rather the principal delight of her day was the ceaseless dance of flirtation – frissons with the postman, the bus driver, the boy in the sandwich shop. And so to find herself intent on charming a stranger on the bus this Monday morning was really no surprise.

She took out her lipstick and her compact and made a show of repainting herself. Then, as she returned the make-up to her bag, she dropped her magazine into the aisle between them. Danny had seen it all out of the corner of his eye, and in truth it had both faintly amused and vaguely repulsed him. He turned now to see her stretching to retrieve her magazine, the cleavage thrust forward, eyes peering up at him expectantly. His hand reached the magazine at the same moment as hers and she giggled.

'Thank you,' she mouthed, and gave him a look that was half invitation, half challenge.

'No problem,' he told her blankly, reaching into his bag and taking out his library copy of *The Wild Palms*; it was a retaliation, he felt, against her cheap fashion magazine, with its glossy pages and dead-eyed models and endless list of things to buy.

Terri stared at the floor, at the small sample sachet of

perfume that had slipped from her magazine pages and now rested at his feet. Already some of the day's thrill seemed to have evaporated. She lifted her magazine in defeat.

In a town this small, lives are always certain to overlap. Routines intersect on bus routes and railway stations, in chip shop queues and public toilets; faces grow familiar, neighbours grow accustomed to the sound of one another's footsteps, they exchange their morning greet-ings, set their clocks by the sound of car engines starting. And amid this well-set familiarity, anomalies will stick out like loose shingle: unknown faces on buses, lipstick on collars, unexpected scents on a lover's skin.

Terri had known Jeannie's face long before she had connected it to Jimmy. She was a regular customer at the perfume counter, a great believer in cleansing masks and firming lotions, eye serums and foot files.

Later, when she had discovered that the mouse of a girl at Pemberton's was her rival for Jimmy's affections she had been quite astounded. The very same day, she had visited the counter under the ruse of needing more toner and inspected Jeannie more closely. She was a little appalled by the girl's dowdy figure and unkempt hair, by her scraggy fingernails and the pink lipstick that looked to have been rather hastily applied. Most of all it perplexed her that there was nothing about this girl that sparkled. She bagged up the toner and talked Terri through the special gift offers with no more animation than if she were detailing the best route to take to Preston.

Jimmy, Terri felt, deserved more than that. Her attraction to him had been immediate; he was tall and sturdily built, and his voice was deep and broad, and there was something about him that belonged to this place, as if he were built out of the same heavy red brick as its terraces. Terri was rooted here too; her brief time away from the town had kindled in her a yearning for its roads and its rivers, an unquenchable thirst for northern light. And so her feelings for Jimmy were in some way knitted to her unbridled love for the town itself.

They were both regulars at the pub, part of the same gang, with their usual table by the fireplace, their in-jokes and their intimate knowledge of everyone's drink and routine. Terri couldn't help but feel that whenever Jeannie joined them she brought with her a cold-weather front, sitting quiet and awkward beside Jimmy, pestering him to ease up on the lager, to go home early. She was a damp leaf that clung to him.

Today, put out by the fact that the man on the bus had so casually rebuffed her advances, she felt the desire to recover her pride. And so she stayed in her seat all the way to the bus station and headed in the direction of Pemberton's. It was a bolstering sort of day. The breeze lifted the hem of her dress, her heels struck the pavement with a satisfying clack, and she sailed through the doors of the department store like a small blonde galleon; shoulders back, skirt billowing, blonde hair bouncing a little as she charged down the aisles of the perfume hall. She came to a halt at the St Emmanuelle counter, where Jeannie was restocking the jar of cotton-wool balls.

'Hi!' Terri called. Her voice had a waltz to it. She pressed her fingertips against the counter-top, chest heaving forward, nails an immaculate red. 'How are you, Jeannie? Not long till the big day now, is it?'

Jeannie stood looking discombobulated, both hands full of cotton balls. She was not fond of Terri.

'Oh I'm well,' she assured her, and dug her fingers into the cotton wool. 'You're looking very summery!' she added, because quite unmistakably there was something different about Terri today, as if her brassiness rang a little louder than normal.

'Well I've got a new fella,' Terri told her, with what might have been a smirk. 'And you know what they say, a woman always looks her most beautiful when she's in love!'

Jeannie smiled stiffly. 'So I've heard. Who is the lucky guy?'

'Ohhhh,' Terri feigned coyness. 'You know him, actually … But we're keeping it a bit hush-hush for now.' Her eyes met Jeannie's and seemed to rest there for a moment. 'I'm sure it'll all come out eventually,' she said, and then she looked down at the counter, swept her eyes over the lipsticks and blushers and eyeshadow palettes. 'So I'm after a new perfume,' she added.

That summer, St Emmanuelle had released a new fragrance they named Miss Emmanuelle. It was the product of intensive research over the course of five years at the St Emmanuelle laboratories in Cincinnati. It was packaged in a pink embossed box, its name in gold letters, and the bottle itself was frosted pink glass with a gold trim. While many of the fragrances launched at this time were cleaner and crisper and more unisex than their predecessors, there was an old-fashioned quality to Miss Emmanuelle: it was girly and romantic, sensual and seductive, a marriage of freesia and rose, heliotrope and magnolia, vanilla and musk. The advertising campaign showed a popular Hollywood actress wrapped in layers of soft pink organza, wearing nothing but a pair of gold stilettos.

Terri picked up the pink bottle and shuffled out the stopper. 'I heard an advert for this on the radio,' she said, and sniffed the perfume. 'Oh I like that,' she cooed, and sniffed again. 'That's a proper perfume, that.'

'You should try it on your wrist,' Jeannie told her. 'See how it settles on your skin.'

Terri dabbed on the Miss Emmanuelle and pressed her wrist up to her nose. 'Oh that's lovely,' she declared, and offered her arm to Jeannie for inspection.

Jeannie breathed in the strong rush of perfume mingling with the scent of Terri's skin. She did not like Miss Emmanuelle any better than she liked Terri. It was a heavy fragrance, too synthetic and too cloying for her liking, and it seemed to grab at everything that passed: to clutch your wrist and cling to your clothes, to wrap itself around you and tug at your sleeve like a needy child.

'Not a scent you'd forget, that, is it?' said Terri, wafting her arm a little in the air and sniffing her wrist again. 'I'll take a bottle of the eau de toilette, and the body lotion too. I like to layer a perfume. Lasts longer that way, doesn't it? That's what I read in a magazine once.'

Later that night, and in the nights that followed, Jeannie would feel the constant, tugging scent of Miss Emmanuelle; it filled her nostrils as she slept, and seemed to crawl about the house, winding its way around the furnishings and in amongst the curtains. She would wash and rewash her hands, her hair, the bed linen to escape it. But still it gripped on, a nagging reminder of Terri, standing at the perfume counter with her brassiness and her cleavage and her talk of a new man.

Jimmy smelled it when Terri answered the door that evening, as he stood in the hallway and pressed his face into her neck he drew it in, tasted it on his tongue, on his lips. She smelled exquisite, he thought, heavy and rich and womanly, and he lost himself in the scent of her skin and the waves of her hair and the soft folds of her dress.

'You can't marry her, Jimmy,' she clucked. His hands were halfway to her knickers, and his face was deep in the warm crevice of her neck, and all thought of getting married on Saturday had been lost somewhere in the scent of rose and vanilla and musk.

'Mhmm,' he said, neither no nor yes, but a breathy acknowledgement that something had been said.

'I'm serious,' she said, a little louder now, pulling her body, her scented skin away from him. 'You can't marry her, because she won't make you happy. I'll make you happy, and I'm right here and I'll be yours, but I can't be yours if you marry her.'

Jimmy was of course a practical man, and his instincts told him to deal with the matter now immediately before him rather than address the root problem. He would say anything, he believed, to halt this gushing sense of panic, to put a halt to whatever it was that might prevent him from carrying Terri upstairs and taking off this pretty summer dress she wore. It was much the same feeling as dealing with a burst pipe; the first thing to do was to turn off the stop tap.

'I know, sweetheart,' he muttered, and pulled her body towards him again. He felt her waist strain.

'Seriously, Jimmy,' she said, and her breath brushed

his cheek, smelling of warm, sweet wine. 'I can't be your bit on the side.'

Jimmy ran his hand up her thigh and over her hip, paused to admire the curve of her. 'I know, I know,' he said, his hand edging up to her chest.

'Promise me you won't marry her?' she demanded, as his fingers pulled at the strap of her dress. 'Promise me?'

He pushed his face back into the warm crease of her neck. 'I promise,' he murmured, not knowing whether he promised or not. 'I promise.'

The plan, Terri told him, was simple. She was naked beside him in her big brass bed, with the sheet twined up strategically to just below her breasts, while Jimmy was rolling a cigarette listening to the rise and fall of her voice. On Saturday morning, early, he would call Jeannie at her parents' home and break the news to her. He would tell her it had all been a big mistake, and that he was sorry but he had come to realise that he couldn't marry her. Then in the afternoon he would drive over here to Terri's house, where she would be waiting with her bags all packed, and together they would drive to her uncle's holiday cottage in Anglesey, lie low for a couple of weeks until it all blew over a bit. She scratched her thigh. 'How d'you think she'll take it?' she asked him.

He thought of Jeannie, called to the phone on the

morning of her wedding, standing in the hallway beside the framed family photographs and the watercolour painting of Lake Windermere. He thought of the light through the front door, of her pale, rough hands cradling the receiver, and his belly lurched just a little. He tried to picture her face, tried to imagine how her eyes might fall, how her mouth might crumple and twist, but as hard as he tried, he could not see it.

'She'll be OK,' he said quietly. 'She'll be all right,' he added, as much to himself as to her.

Terri was swept up in it all now. There was, she admitted to herself, no real reason to convince Jimmy of delaying the announcement until the morning of the wedding, except that the drama of it was so thrilling. She traced her finger across his chest.

'You won't back out, will you, Jimmy? You won't let me down?' She looked up at him, all blue eyes and soft voice and warm, naked skin.

He drew on his cigarette, exhaled slowly through his nose, and twirled one pale lock of hair around his finger.

'No, sweetheart,' he said, 'I won't let you down.'

The foils made a sound like tiny bursts of thunder as they shook, and as each strip drew close, Jeannie watched her face bulge and balloon in its reflection. The hairdresser kept a small pile of silver strips at her elbow as she worked, turning to lift the bowl and brush, working the bleach into dry strands, wrapping the foils around. It was the girls at work who had suggested it. 'Just a few highlights,' said April, 'just to lift the colour a bit.' 'Just to bring out your eyes,' Michaela nodded, and wrote down the name of a salon in the arcade. 'Just like you've been in the sunshine,' the hairdresser said now, and then she positioned the heater and set a heavy pile of magazines on Jeannie's lap. 'Thirty minutes,' she said.

The magazines had all been read into tattiness, their pages creased and stained, and when Jeannie leafed through them she saw how the fashion spreads looked unseasonal, and the word-searches had all been completed, in various shades of ballpoint pen. From time to time a page had been ripped out, leaving only a half-finished article and a fray of paper along the spine. She turned to the problem page and looked at the headlines. *My Boyfriend Won't Commit*, she read. *I'm Having Another Man's Baby. Is My Husband Having an Affair?* She felt heavy, suddenly, weighted down by all these faceless, nameless people; everyone worrying over variations on the same old theme: Do I love him? Does he love me?

She stared at herself in the mirror. In the salon gown and foils she thought she looked oddly surgical, and her face seemed somehow unfamiliar. This was the thing, she thought, as she took in the features that looked harder, sharper than she had believed them to be: she had become a person she didn't recognise, a person who lied and was selfish and unkind. Her grey eyes looked colder, even, and her mouth was set in a hard, short line, lips sealed lest they spill secrets.

'That temperature OK?' the junior asked. Jeannie was head-back in the basin, lukewarm water raking her scalp. She nodded. She had never quite fathomed the etiquette of hairdressing salons; there were so many questions – about water temperature and conditioner on ends and would she like a head massage or a cup of tea? And all the while other women strayed between the sinks and the mirrors looking frail and disorientated in their long salon gowns; their hair bundled in bleach-speckled towels, their hands clutching their bags. There was something of the convalescent about them as they walked. Jeannie yawned as the junior dried her hair, enjoyed the warm air against her neck, and when she looked up she saw that she looked like a house repainted; her drab old hair replaced by a bright new gaudiness. Only her pale skin looked familiar, and that, too, would soon disappear beneath a layer of fake tan.

She sat on the bank by the tippler, waiting for Danny to arrive. The paving stones were warm beneath her thighs, and the canal looked pretty in the early evening sun, yellowed grass floating close to the banks, ducks meandering up to the Pottery Changeline. The water was shadowed by the old warehouses that still ran along these banks, that made offices now, and space for bulk storage, a theme pub, a nightclub, a museum. The tippler itself was not the original. That disappeared years ago, sold as scrap iron after the old staithe came down, but subsequently replaced with a replica for the tourist trade.

This was where the wagons had once rolled in, where they'd come right up to the water's brink before tipping their load of coal into the waiting barge, feeding the boats, keeping the engines firing. It formed little more than a raised point on the bank these days, the cobbles sloping briefly upwards to a small wooden platform and two black metal curves. Behind the tippler now stood a red brick wall, plumed with barbed wire, and beyond that several low warehouse buildings with corrugated roofs and hand-painted hoardings promising car sales and budget exhausts.

She studied a strand of hair, tugged at the two fine branches of a rogue split end. There were so many ways to break up with someone, she thought: a letter, a phone call, leaving them alone at the altar, alone in a railway buffet. She twisted the strand of hair until it snapped.

With Danny she had the feeling of trying something on for size, of visiting a dress boutique and putting on an outfit for which she had no occasion, of pretending that she was someone she wasn't. And there were times, too, when she wondered if the person she had fallen for wasn't Danny at all but her new and interesting self.

Either way, she worried that if she got married on Saturday she would lose them both.

But in truth she knew it was probably too late to change her mind. All those months of engagement, the rings chosen, the dresses, the flowers, the cake; the speeches written, the cars booked, the women who on Saturday morning would be blowing up balloons and decorating the club with strings of crepe paper. And her mother, who over these last few months had tried to sow her excitement into the purchase of hats and sachets of confetti, into the posting of invitations and the collating of numbers, but Jeannie knew the excitement was there, buried away, quietly growing. It felt like the end of the summer holidays, as if the days would soon grow colder and shorter. Danny had been a summer, she told herself, just a long, sweet stretch of un-uniformed freedom.

She heard him approach, his footsteps padding down the flight of stairs, his boots scuffling the path. She was filled then with a great wash of sadness, the thought that this might be the last time she saw him. After all, the rest of the week was cluttered with wedding prepara- tions which would leave little time for visits to the railway buffet, or to sit and while away the evening on warm embankments.

'Isn't this an evening?' he said, and dropped his bag down beside her in a cloud of summer dust. 'Christ!

You've gone blonde!' He slumped on to the pavement beside her and brushed his hand over her new hair. 'I like it,' he lied.

'Just fancied a change,' she answered. Her voice sounded high and thin, a balloon deflating. 'I got us some beers,' she told him, and busied herself unlidding two bottles of Guinness with her door key.

'Aren't you a treasure!' he told her, and she half-laughed, half-hiccoughed, and took a long swig of stout, throwing her neck back and scrunching her eyes in the hope that gravity might convince the gathering tears to retreat. The Guinness tasted good: cool and flat and earthy against her scratchy throat.

He told her about the scandal at the railway station, the weekend vandals who had spray-painted expletives all across the walls of the gentlemen's toilets. The word 'fuck' written in silver, twelve inches high, above the basins. She told him about Miss Emmanuelle, about the pink and gold box and the women who flocked to the counter to buy it. In a week, she assured him, the whole town would carry the stench of rose and musk and heliotrope.

'So I've been thinking,' he said, peeling the label from the damp, dark bottle. 'What are you doing on Saturday?'

Jeannie looked at the ducks, far away now, only their tails bobbing near the bridge. 'I don't know,' she lied.

'Because I was thinking, we should go somewhere. Not a daytrip, I mean really go, you and me.'

She didn't reply. He stared at her, waiting for her to say something, to laugh even, to tell him not to be so daft, but instead she kept her eyes steady on her hands, holding the cold bottle of stout.

Somewhere in her belly, Jeannie felt the words shift and take shape, they rose halfway and then stuck in her chest. Now was the time to tell him that it was too late, that she was engaged to another man, that she had always been engaged, and that while she could not explain herself, or expect him to forgive her, she did love him.

Instead she opened her mouth just a little, breathed in the taste of stout and canal air, the fumes from the road, and then she lifted the bottle to her mouth, pressed the cold glass to her lips and downed the rest of her Guinness.

'Is that a yes?' he wondered.

'Where would we go?' she asked. She felt a little sick now.

'South somewhere,' he said. 'To the sea, maybe. Or we could go to Kent and pick fruit. Or anywhere really. Anywhere you want.'

She said nothing. He fiddled with the beer label, nervous hands folding it into a small, sleek aeroplane.

'I thought we could go Saturday afternoon,' he said, 'you could meet me at the station and we could just catch the train, we could just leave, together.' He looked at her, sitting beside him, blonde hair hanging over her face, seeming to be just on the brink of saying something. 'Will you?' he asked. 'Will you go with me?'

'Yes,' she answered quietly, and with one hand she reached out and touched the tippler, felt her life fall over into the darkness.

Chapter Eleven

The bus paused by Gaskell's Mill, and from under the chassis the air huffed against the pavement, warm and heavy with diesel fumes. Late afternoon, and Jeannie was making her way out of town, watching the buildings that lined the route shift from shopfronts to warehouses and factories and disused mills. There was a drab feeling around here now, and though the buildings stood tall and broad, it had acquired a flatness, as when land gives way to the sea.

She remembered a school trip here once, a visit to the mill museum for home economics class. The mill stood five storeys high, and in its belly lay the steam engine itself: seventy tonnes, four cylinders, 2,500 horse-power. The class had fidgeted and laughed as they toured the factory floor, their voices had risen up in squeals and whispers and stifled giggles as the guide spoke of ring spinning and pirn winders and the north light swimming down to keep the weavers cool.

But they had fallen silent when the engine was switched on, when it roared and it screamed and the room shook and juddered and the air itself seemed to rattle. They had stood and watched the beast spring to life, with all its pulleys and cylinders and pumps, the churn of the flywheel, and the piston rods thrusting like the hind legs of a grasshopper. Their faces had paled and their mouths had dropped open, mesmerised by the terrifying rush of the past.

The lesson itself she struggled to remember now, but looking up at the familiar bulk of the mill this afternoon she thought it must have been some sort of introduction to the industrial revolution, to the history of textile manufacturing, to the story of spinning and weaving in the North-West. They were hand-weavers first, working at home, and then in small groups, and later at the machines in the factories. It seemed sometimes as if the cotton industry covered this part of the world like some vast bus network, an invisible web of routes and connections, its threads entwined and interlocked, the residents united by an unspoken familiarity with its workings.

The last of the town's mills closed fifteen years ago now. Gaskell's ceased production well before that, but it had remained a landmark in the town, a reminder of their collective past. Though it had never called in her lifetime, Jeannie knew the sound of the mill hooter, the cold, deep, dark howl that clung to your bones. She knew the clamour of the looms, and the weavers' songs, knew how the Lancashire looms used just one shuttle and how they could weave only the plainest fabric – grey cloth, they called it – that would be transported elsewhere to be bleached and printed. And the grey cloth seemed fitting; sometimes even now it looked as if the days and the sky and the people themselves had been woven out of the same grey cotton calico.

As the doors hissed closed and the bus pulled away from the kerb, she was still thinking of those home economics lessons: of the stitches practised on coarse scraps of twill, blanket and satin stitch, cross stitch and running stitch; the lessons in home-making, the baking of sausage rolls and apricot flans; the rudimentaries of dressmaking and food hygiene; the long afternoons spent plotting the path from cottonflower to poplin. All those hours learning about how they made jacquard and grosgrain and Harris tweed, the art of fine damask.

The bus paused at the junction, hoping for a break in the traffic. The cars sailed north and sailed south, and as she watched them pass, Jeannie was half-remembering a lesson about shedding, about the process of dividing the warp into two strands so that the weft could pass between them, carried by the shuttle that flew through the gap. It was all about looking for a gap, she thought as the bus pulled out, continuing on its journey eastward; it was all about finding a space through which you could fly. She could feel the taste of flight on her tongue as she thought it, and as she considered the hours that now stretched to her marriage, it seemed there was still the smallest perceivable gap through which she too might slip.

It was the evening before her wedding day, and the town was succumbing to the charms of Friday night. Yesterday had been her last day at Pemberton's before the wedding, and at closing time the girls in the perfume department had presented her with a gift-wrapped box. She had pulled at the purple satin ribbon, lifted the lid and found inside a fancy lingerie set nestled against peach tissue paper.

'For your honeymoon,' winked Michaela, and Jeannie had blushed and bobbed her head and traced a hand over the fine black lace. Today she had been caught up in a scurry of last-minute preparations: nails to be painted, telephone calls to be made, items to be collected from town. Late in the afternoon she had stopped by the railway station, stood on her tiptoes and kissed Danny on the lips while her bridal veil sat in its stiff cardboard bag by her ankles.

He gripped her hand. 'All packed for tomorrow?' he asked. She nodded. And it was strange, because even now she did not quite believe she would not board the train with him. In the emptiness of the station buffet, she cupped his face and nuzzled his neck and pressed her cheek against his warm, freckled skin.

To Danny, it showed a depth of affection, a new and certain devotion. To Jeannie these were the slow acts of parting, the start of the letting go, pressing the memory of someone's skin, someone's scent, into your own.

She looked at him, took in those steady blue eyes, the warm, leaf-mould hue of his hair, and she kissed him goodbye, tasted the coffee on his breath, breathed in the soapy fragrance of his shirt collar.

'See you tomorrow,' he told her, and she stood in the door, and smiled.

'Yes,' she said. 'See you tomorrow.'

And as she walked slowly down the steps, she tried to remember every bit of it, the sound of her soles striking the lip of the stair, the warm, damp smell of the underpass, collecting the details so that she might look at them later, a bag of mementos in her pocket. Then outside the station she had boarded a bus to her grandmother's house.

Her grandmother was standing at the window, watching the birds in the back garden. She turned as Jeannie came in, and the light caught her hair, set back from her forehead in fine, colourless waves. In that moment she saw her grandmother's face as it must have been when she was young, a glimpse of her mother's face, and also her own, and then the light settled on the translucent blue folds of her eyelids and the yellowish cast to the whites.

'They come back every year,' her grandmother was saying, raising her hand to the windowpane. 'They always come back!' Jeannie saw that she was pointing at a pair of blackbirds in the garden.

She stood alongside her and looked through the glass to where the birds were busying themselves. The female was a rich shade of brown, a smaller, meeker-looking creature, bobbing her bill towards the ground, hunting for insects and earthworms while her companion sat on the washing-line post and sang.

'Where are they nesting?' Jeannie asked.

'In the ivy, up against the wall there,' her grandmother said proudly. 'I went out and took a look today. You can barely see it – it's just a little cup of a nest, all grass and mud.'

They listened to the male singing from his post. 'I do love that sound,' her grandmother said. 'And he's bold as brass too. I was out in the garden today and he was right by me as I pegged out the washing: singing away he was. I thought to myself I've lived in this house ever since I was first married to your grandfather – I've raised a family here, seen them grow up and have their own families, seen your grandfather pass, seen a lot of people pass, and I've seen this road change, I've watched them put in fishponds and conservatories and double-glazing and gas pipes all down the street, and the neighbours have come and gone, and the shops are different, and the fashions are different, and I dare say I look different too,' she smiled and touched her hair. 'But every year the blackbirds have always been here, just the same, and I've been listening to that same song, that same blackbird song, every year. And every year when I first hear it in the spring, I think to myself how there's nowhere I would rather be so much as right here.'

They stood in silence, side by side, watching the garden. The blackbird was still singing, his beak a sharp yellow in the early evening light, and his throat pulsing and fluttering with the notes. Her grandmother looked at Jeannie, put an arm around her. 'Anyway, love, you didn't come here to talk about blackbirds. Let's put the kettle on, shall we?' she said, and she guided her granddaughter through to the kitchen.

'Are you excited about tomorrow?' she asked as she turned the tap, and her eyes lifted to the kitchen window, sought out the blackbirds again.

'Yes, I suppose so,' Jeannie answered, though her voice was flat.

Her grandmother heaved the kettle to the hob, there came the brief flare and fizzle of the gas, and then she warmed the pot, opened the tea caddy, found cups and milk.

'Well,' she said eventually. 'No doubt you're nervous too.'

'Yes,' Jeannie said, and she fiddled with the hem of her T-shirt, folding it in small pleats against her index finger.

'You should have seen me the night before I got married.' Her grandmother smiled and sat down at the table. 'My mother was ready to call the doctor!'

Jeannie smiled. Her grandmother still kept her wedding picture on the mantelpiece, and oftentimes in the last few months Jeannie had taken it down to look at it closely, to try to discern just what she had been feeling on that day. She seemed so serene in her long cream dress and veil, standing on the church steps arm in arm with her new husband, her face still and sweet and pale. But it was her eyes that gave her away – there was a wildness to them, a look that was somewhere between triumph and fear.

'Were you nervous?' she asked.

'Well it was different then,' her grandmother said, folding her hands on the table. 'I was scared to death! And so naïve! I'd never seen your grandfather, or any man, for that matter, without his clothes. My mother sat me down the night before my wedding and told me what was expected of me.'

She started to laugh, a faint wheezy chuckle that began in her chest and seemed to spread right up to her eyes.

'I don't imagine your mother will have need to do that …'
she said. 'But of course marriage was different then too.
It wasn't so much this fairytale. It was for life, and it was
a thing that you worked at, together. People have such
expectations now.'

Jeannie chewed her lip.

'And you should have seen your mother!' her grandmother continued. 'Oh, she was a state! Railing about
how she didn't love him and she hated her dress and she'd
wasted her life …'

'Really?'

'Oh yes.' She patted Jeannie's hands. 'It goes on,' she
said. 'It just keeps on rolling on and on, this great long
thread. One day you'll have a daughter, and she'll be just
the same; we're all strung together, aren't we?'

Jeannie sat quietly and listened to the kettle gathering
speed. She felt chastened. Her fears were no different to
those of any other bride, yet she had buckled, she had
wanted the fairytale and she had been weak and dallied
with someone else. She thought of Danny's face, thought
of the taste of him and the scent of him, of the warmth
of her hand in his. It was only a silly idea of love.

She watched her grandmother stand and lift the kettle,
thought of the years she had spent with her grandfather,
growing together. And now everything that she had with
Jimmy, all the years that they had spent together, seemed
tainted.

'Can I use your phone, Grandma?' she asked. She had a sudden desire to hear Jimmy's voice, to apologise.

'Of course, dear,' her grandmother said, and Jeannie pushed back her chair and hurried through to the hall.

Her fingers dialled her own number. Jimmy would be home by now. She listened to the line ringing out, and as she listened she thought of how this was where she belonged — not on a train to London with a boy she barely knew. And she thought of that long thread, how finely it hung between the generations, and how, when the cotton used to break on the looms, the thread had to be pieced. This, she told herself, was what she was doing now: piecing things back together.

Her heart beat against her chest, pulsed and fluttered like the throat of the blackbird.

Jimmy came to the phone a little breathless.

'Hello?' he blurted.

'You're there!' Jeannie said, relieved. She could hear noise in the background, music playing or a television set.

'Jeannie?' Jimmy said. 'You OK?'

'Yes, I just …' Her voice seemed to snag and then run. 'I just wanted to speak to you.'

'Are you at your mam's?' he asked.

'No, I'm round my nan's, and I just wanted to tell you I love you and that I can't wait to see you tomorrow.' She bit her lip. It was the most romantic thing she had ever said to Jimmy, and the words felt a little awkward, as if she had borrowed somebody else's shoes.

There was a pause down the line. 'Well I love you too, sweetheart,' Jimmy said quietly.

'OK,' Jeannie said softly. She felt a great rush of warmth and sorrow and fondness, a tenderness even for the way he ate his cereal, for the way that he looked asleep in the morning with his hair all smudged and tousled on the pillow and the gentle huff of his breath against the sheets. 'Well, I'll see you tomorrow,' she told him.

'You will,' he replied. 'Sleep tight, love.'

Jeannie listened to the line click as he replaced the receiver, heard the dial tone spring up. And yet she stood quite still in the hallway, still cradling the phone, pressing it against her ear. 'I'm sorry,' she said down the line, though there was no one left to hear her. 'I'm sorry.'

Jimmy stood by the phone table and rested his head against the wall. The hallway was decorated with an embossed paper that had been painted over with heavy white gloss. He was rather glad of this fact just now, of the way the wall pressed cool and firm against his hot forehead. Dear God, he thought to himself, he had got into a right old mess now.

'Jimmy?' Terri's voice called through from the lounge.

He sighed. It was one thing, he realised, to play away

from home, but it was quite another to play away in your own home.

Terri had come round after work, and it was a mixture of surprise and lust that had led him to invite her in. Then she had stood in the lounge and looked around, lifting up ornaments and opening drawers while he opened a bottle of wine. She had asked the way to the bathroom and he had heard her upstairs, opening cabinets, and padding her way across the landing to inspect the bedroom. By the time she returned downstairs he had knocked back a glass of wine just to steady his nerves.

It had seemed best, he decided, to get this over with quickly: to screw her there in the lounge then put her in a taxi home. If he played it right, he thought, he could have her out the door by half nine, which would still leave plenty of time for him to puzzle out just what on earth he was going to do tomorrow.

Now he stood up, wiped his hand across his face and walked back through to the lounge, to where Terri lay on the sofa with her skirt hitched up, her knickers blooming like a pink satin rosette on the carpet.

'Who was it?' she asked.

'No one important,' he said, and then winced. 'I mean, you know, it doesn't matter.' He bent down and kissed her, partly because he wanted to, and partly because he didn't want her to ask any more questions.

He was kissing her soft warm neck when Terri pushed

her mouth right up to his ear. 'Let's go upstairs,' she demanded.

Jimmy paused. This was a bad idea. 'No,' he told her. 'Let's do it here.'

'Why here?' she asked, though she knew the answer. He sensed a determination to her voice, even to the way her body moved beneath him.

He ran his hands up her thighs, hoping to distract her. 'Why not here?'

'Come on, Jimmy,' Terri said bluntly, 'I want you to prove I'm more to you than she is.'

Jimmy sat up. There was no way out, he saw that now. 'All right, OK,' he said, and held out his hand to help her up. If this had to happen, he told himself, he should at least get it over and done with. He glanced at his watch. He was still making good time.

He watched her smooth, plump thighs as he climbed the stairs behind her, and decided that this was not after all, the worst thing to be happening. In the bedroom, Terri turned the lights on and left the curtains open, pushed Jimmy up against the bed. It was still light outside, and as he rested his head against the pillows and felt her unzipping his jeans he looked out across the street, at the birds cutting across the evening sky and the familiar view of rooftops and chimney-stacks, all lit up by the fading light. He was still watching the houses across the street as she straddled him, and he looked past her hips to see a light come on in an upstairs room, watched a figure move behind the net curtains, wondered what this Friday night had brought for them.

'I love you, Jimmy,' Terri told him, and he looked up at her, traced a hand over her breasts, felt her skin warm and clammy.

'I love you too,' he said, and she smiled.

'Really?' she asked.

'Really,' he replied.

Did he really love her? He had, in the space of half an hour, told two different women that he loved them both, when in truth he was not entirely sure he loved either. He thought of Jeannie, her voice faint and strained down the line from her grandmother's house, and he thought of how the feeling he had for her was so warm and familial.

And here was Terri, a gleam of conquest in her eyes as she screwed him in his marital bed. And yet at this moment he felt strangely removed from the experience. She looked faintly ridiculous, he thought, bobbing away on top of him, bleating and wailing theatrically. He smiled in a way that he hoped was encouraging but in fact owed more to relief. At this rate, he thought, she might even be out of the door by nine o'clock.

'Come with me,' Terri demanded, knotting her hands in his, looking him dead in the eye. Jimmy blanched. He had never faked an orgasm in his life. And yet he felt so thoroughly disengaged from the woman writhing around on top of him that at this moment there really seemed no other choice. Would she be able to tell, he wondered? He closed his eyes and tried to think of something erotic. He thought of Angelica, the garage calendar girl.

'Look at me, Jimmy,' Terri insisted, and he sprung his eyes open to see her face close to his, her damp hair sticking to her forehead, her cheeks flushed, her breath heavy. 'I love you,' she told him again, 'I love you.' Jimmy closed his eyes and waited until it was over.

Around half past six, just as the local news began, Jeannie pulled on her jacket. 'Well, I'd best be off home, Nan,' she said above the blare of the television set. 'Else I'll be late for my tea.'

Her grandmother nodded and looked up from the screen. 'Jeannie love,' she said, fiddling for the volume button on the remote. 'No matter how nervous you are now, tomorrow will be the best day of your life. And we'll all be there, and you'll look beautiful, and Jimmy will be a very happy man.'

Jeannie nodded and forced a smile. 'Thanks, Grandma.' She leant down and kissed her cheek. 'I'll see you tomorrow.'

It was still warm out, and Jeannie walked to her parents' house, enjoying the brush of evening air against her bare legs. She wondered what Jimmy was doing, and she wondered where Danny might be, and as she walked along the pavement doubt seemed to creep between the cracks in her thoughts. She was halfway home when she passed the phone box, and almost on a whim she heaved open the heavy red door and stepped inside. It smelled of urine and cigarette smoke and the floor was specked with chewing-gum wrappers, crisp packets, grubby scraps of paper. She pushed a twenty pence piece into the slot and punched in Marie's number.

'Hey it's me,' she told her. 'You busy?'

'Never too busy for the bride,' Marie laughed.

Jeannie smiled. 'Come walk around the block with me?' she asked.

'Course,' Marie said. 'See you by the shop in two.'

She arrived brandishing two blue ice pops. 'For the good old days,' she said. They had spent most of their teenage years walking these streets eating blue ice pops, talking about boys.

'This'll be us,' Marie said as they set off along the Billinge Road, 'thirty years from now, still walking around these streets, still eating ice pops, gossiping about our husbands and our kids.'

'D'you really reckon so?' Jeannie asked.

'Well I'm not planning on going anywhere, are you?' Marie asked, her teeth gnawing at the plastic. 'So unless they stop making ice pops, I reckon we've got the next thirty years all planned out for us.'

Jeannie numbed her lips against the ice. 'I don't know that I'm doing the right thing,' she said after a moment or two. 'I mean marrying Jimmy. Is that the right thing?'

Marie slid her eyes to the left and took in her best friend. 'What makes you think it's not?'

'Just …' Jeannie shrugged. 'Is this it? How do I know this is it? What have I measured it against, you know? Much as I love walking these streets eating ice pops, do I really want to do that for ever?'

'I'll try not to take that personally,' Marie said.

'Oh no, no, you know what I mean.' Jeannie shook her head and waved her free hand and Marie laughed.

'I do know,' she said. 'But I also I think you can go around the world and sow your wild oats and whatever, but will it make you any happier? I just think maybe the more you see, the more you want.'

They walked in silence, turned the corner, headed into the belly of the estate. There were children playing out in the street, chasing one another with water bombs, shrieking and squealing with delight.

'I don't know if I love him,' Jeannie said. 'I don't know if I've ever actually loved him.'

'What?' Marie stopped on the pavement. 'Jeannie, that is fucking ridiculous.' Her voice startled them both. 'I was with you when you first met him. And I was with you when you used to get dressed up and mope around the football pitch just to catch a glimpse of him. And it was me he asked to ask you out. I helped you choose his Valentine's Day cards, I told your mum you were staying at ours so you could slope off to his house, and I've sat on the end of that telephone and listened to you going on and on about Jimmy pretty much every day since the very first time you set your cap at him. So don't try and tell me you don't love him.'

Jeannie stared at her shoes.

'Over there, look.' Marie stood with her hand on her hip and nodded at the children's playground on the edge of the park. 'I remember being sixteen years old and you and Jimmy sitting on that roundabout snogging and me hoping that one day I'd fall in love like that.'

Jeannie remembered it too, that summer, sixteen and a hive of hormones, the days when it seemed physically to hurt to be away from him for even a moment.

'And I remember,' Marie ploughed on, 'I remember Jimmy practically carrying you up this street after you got drunk on Buckfast, and you threw up all over his shirt, and he said it didn't matter because he loved you more than he loved his shirt. Don't you remember that?'

Jeannie nodded meekly.

'The thing is, Jeannie, we grow up. We're not teenagers any more. We get jobs and we get married, and we squabble over who does the washing up, and we moan about their stinking football socks and the fact they never make the bed, and they see us in the mornings when we've not done our make-up and we've not brushed our hair and we don't smell as sweet as they'd like. It doesn't mean we've fallen out of love with each other, it just means that love changes, it gets a little softer, spreads out and settles down a bit, you know? It's got to get comfortable because we're in it for the long haul.' Marie stopped. 'Do you get what I mean?'

'Yes,' Jeannie said quietly.

Marie shook her head. 'You know what I think?' she asked, scrunching the remnants of her ice pop. 'I think your brain's been poisoned by those sodding wedding magazines.'

That night Jeannie lay awake in her childhood bedroom, under her old pink duvet cover in her old single bed. She had forgotten how thin the curtains were, how the light pressed through to pick out the shape of the dressing table and the chair, the teen romance novels lined up on the shelf, the collection of perfume bottles she had accumulated over the years. If she squinted, she could still make out the old posters pinned to the wall, and the wardrobe doors, scarred by stickers of boy-bands and Hollywood heart-throbs.

Marie, she realised, was right: she had been crazy about Jimmy once. She had talked for hours about the way he brushed his hair from his eyes, about his love for Panda Cola and Black Jacks. The thrill she felt now when she looked at the freckles on Danny's arms was really no different to how she had once felt about Jimmy's smile: a sudden blooming in her chest, a rush of blood to her face.

And so what would happen, she speculated, if she did board that train with Danny tomorrow? What if a couple of years down the line she grew tired of the way he was too, what if it started to niggle her that he was always quoting books at her, telling her to read this or read that, always trying to educate her? What if he never stopped going on about Allen Ginsberg and John Coltrane? What if then she looked around and found another boy with pretty blue eyes and a nice way with words? Would she run off with him then too? Would she keep running away for ever?

Downstairs her parents were watching television, and she heard the show's canned laughter floating up through the floorboards. She was too restless to sleep, and so she propped herself up on her elbows, turned on the lamp and opened her bedside cabinet. Once upon a time she had kept everything important in that cabinet – love letters, trinkets, notes passed in class, later it would be miniatures of vodka, cigarettes, contraceptives.

Now she rummaged about among the jewellery and knick-knacks and old magazines until finally she found what she was looking for – an old diary from that sixteenth summer. There were accounts of afternoons spent kissing in the park, dates to McDonald's, the cinema, bowling, heartfelt protestations of undying love beside exam revision timetables and reminders about birthday parties now long forgotten.

And there, clipped to a day in June, the pictures she had hoped to find: four photographs of the two of them squashed into a photo booth in the market hall. She sat on his knee before a sagging blue curtain, with her arms wrapped about his neck, and in each frame they pulled a different face for the camera – lips curled, or eyes together, or tongues out. And then in the last picture they had kissed. She saw them now, eyelids dipped, lips pressed together, her hand half-buried in his hair, his fingers touching her jaw. What passion they had felt, what love there had been. She ran her finger around their pale young faces, switched off the lamp and lay with the picture still pressed between finger and thumb. The television show theme drifted up the stairs, and in the half-light of her room, sleep settled upon her like a fine white mist.

Chapter Twelve

It rained on the morning of Jeannie's wedding; a familiar grey light pressing through the curtains, a slow, steady ruffle against the windowpane. For a while she lay there listening. The house was rising in a swell of noise: the sound of taps rushing, pipes juddering, a radio playing 'Build Me up Buttercup'.

From where she lay she could see the bag that held her wedding dress hanging on the side of the wardrobe, and even its bulky outline made her chest tighten and her stomach twist.

She felt already quite weary at the prospect of the day; her throat was scratchy and her eyes were sore and sticky with sleep. She sat up, swept back her hair, ran her tongue over her teeth and found them gluey and stale. The strip of passport photos still lay on the pillow beside her, but now they did little to cheer her. Whether it was the rain or her infidelity, it seemed to Jeannie that a grey film now hung over her wedding day, a grubbiness that nothing would remove.

Somewhere across town, Danny would be waking. She pictured his room: the heavy curtains, the pile of books, the warm old-fashioned smell of it. She thought of him rising and bathing and packing his bag, of the scent of new soap on his skin, of the picture in the hall of his grandmother as a newly-wed, so giddy and gleeful and bright.

Her mother knocked briskly at the door and pushed in with a cup of tea and a custard cream. 'Bet you didn't sleep a wink!' she smiled. She was wearing her dressing-gown, a towelled peach robe of uncertain vintage, and as she leant in and kissed her daughter on the forehead, Jeannie could still smell the sleep on her, warm and sweaty and sweet. She parted the curtains, let in a rush of watery light. 'I reckon it'll clear up a bit later,' she said. 'For the photographs.'

Jeannie was busy dissecting the custard cream, prising off the top layer and licking the fondant centre. Her mother sat down heavily on the edge of the bed and smoothed her daughter's hair. 'Your dad's in the shower,' she told her, 'and after he's done you're in next, else

Dannielle'll get in and then we'll all be waiting hours. Karen'll be here to do your hair at half ten, and she says to remind you that no matter what, you haven't to wash it, else it'll never hold. And you should have a piece of toast … it'll be hours till you can eat again.' She cupped Jeannie's face with her right hand and looked her in the eye. 'OK?' she said gently.

The shower squealed and the water thwacked against the curtain. Jeannie slipped out of her nightdress and inspected the orangey tinge to her skin. Yesterday's fake tan had caught in the creases of her elbows, gathered at her knees and her ankles; her hands looked like monkey paws. She sniffed her arm and found it smelled faintly of Ovaltine. It had felt like a strange rite of passage in the beauty salon yesterday – stripped and sloughed and slathered in self-tan, she had felt as if she were finally becoming part of the town: her hair highlighted, her skin tanned. But under it all she knew her real self was hiding, pale, unpolished and drab. She felt like a stage set, like Pemberton's, how gleaming the floors, how sparkling the lights, yet it was only a pretence of glamour, and far away from the shop floor the staff corridors ran faded and dusty and dark. She climbed into the bathtub, stood under the shower and watched the tan run off her body, the water swirling around her brownish feet and away down the drain. The shower ran as hot as she could bear it, and through the steam she admired her toenails, painted softest, quietest pink.

Karen was a slight, well-tanned woman with glossy dark hair that she wore pulled back from her face in a pink satin scrunchie. Though her business was glamour, she exuded an air of taut practicality, much like a school sports teacher. Today she arrived wearing leggings and a pink polo shirt and carrying a large black case stocked with make-up and hairclips and styling mousse. She set a chair in the middle of the lounge and began unpacking the case. 'Now, since you're a bride,' she told Jeannie, 'we're going subtle – we want to be sure your hubby recognises you in church, don't we?' Jeannie nodded. She had the vague feeling that something dreadful was about to take place.

Her mother, Dannielle and Marie were lodged on the sofa drinking tea and looking on. She glanced at Marie and pulled a worried face, the way they used to do across the aisles of the school examination hall. Marie laughed. 'Don't fret, Jeans, we'll make sure you don't look like some Vegas harlot, won't we, Dannielle?'

Jeannie shook her head. 'I'm putting my faith in you and you only, Marie. Dannielle is the closest this street has to a Vegas harlot.'

Dannielle spluttered. 'I am not!' she cried indignantly, and addressed their mother: 'Am I?'

Karen brushed Jeannie's hair ferociously. It was a firm paddle brush with ball-tipped pins that pressed deep against the scalp and it gave off a woomphing sound as it worked.

'You have what I call "difficult" hair, said Karen. Jeannie looked apologetic. 'But I like a challenge,' Karen added and gave a hard, brisk smile. 'And there's nothing a little hairspray and some pins can't master!' Jeannie felt a touch sorry for her hair at that moment, as if it were to be tamed like an unruly horse.

Certainly Karen's approach to hairdressing showed little mercy. She twisted Jeannie's hair back and settled it with a good two dozen pins, then heated her curling tongs and twirled a few strands into long curly ringlets. 'Lovely!' declared her mother, though Jeannie felt faintly jolted, her hair pulled back so tightly that her forehead ached and the sharp points of the hairpins stung her scalp.

Karen rattled the can of hairspray. 'Deep breath!' she commanded, and Jeannie gulped just in time to avoid the hissing cloud of fixative.

Then there seemed to be an endless process of layering: first there was cleansing milk and then toner and then followed moisturiser, after which came primer, which sat for a moment or two while Karen sipped her tea.

'You have to let it set,' she told the audience on the sofa.

Next came foundation, which she applied with a moist sponge shaped like a small wedge of cheese.

'I've never seen that before,' said her mother, approvingly.

'It helps it stay put,' explained Karen, and her breath billowed the scent of sweet tea against Jeannie's face. 'It's all about staying put with wedding make-up,' she continued. 'It's got to go the distance. And it's about the photos too, of course – it's got to look good in the pictures!'

Jeannie slid her eyes to the sofa. Her face had acquired a strange new weight that made her feel as if she were wearing a mask. She looked at Marie, but Marie only smiled reassuringly and nodded. Jeannie remembered now that on Marie's wedding day her face had been painted so heavily that her freckles had entirely disappeared, and when the couple had slow-danced their first song she had left a great tan-coloured smudge on the shoulder of Stephen's suit. She slipped her gaze across to the window, and saw through the nets that the rain had grown heavier.

Karen was powdering her now, blotting her brow and her nose and her chin, while Dannielle told them how she had lined up a date with a policeman. 'He came in the salon,' she explained. 'They'd had some sort of break-in at the offy across the road …'

Jeannie listened instead to Karen sharpening an eyebrow pencil, a steady rasping sound, as if someone in one of the neighbouring streets was planing wood, or shovelling sand, perhaps.

She had no idea what colour Karen was painting her eyes, but she kept them closed – softly, so the lids didn't scrunch, and breathed in the scent of the powder. It was one of the things she liked about Pemberton's, the smell of the make-up, all waxy and dusty and sweet. The newer brands, she noticed, favoured a sharper scent, like wood shavings, but the older perfume houses, of which St Emmanuelle was certainly one, stuck to the heavy, honeyish fragrances. She sprung her eyes open, and found Karen examining her face, brow furrowed, lips pursed, as if contemplating the remaining answers of a crossword puzzle.

As Karen lined her eyes, brushed mascara, curled her lashes, Dannielle was continuing to fill the room with idle chit-chat. Somehow she had reached the story of a friend-of-a-friend who was dating a member of the St John Ambulance brigade. Most likely the connection was uniforms. Jeannie closed her eyes again and let the conversation drift away. She felt as if she were underwater, floating downstream.

'Jeannie?' She heard her mother's voice. 'Jeannie?' She swam to the surface and opened her eyes to find her mother standing above her. 'Telephone!' she said.

The hall smelled of toast and pot-pourri, and the radio spilled through from the kitchen playing some sort of Saturday morning quiz. Jeannie picked up the receiver.

'Hello?' she asked, and her voice sounded high and unfamiliar.

'It's Danny,' came the voice at the end of the line.

'Oh!' she said, startled. 'How did you know where to find me?'

'Phone book,' he said. 'I uh ... well ...' he floundered, and she heard the noises trickling in from the other room – music, women's laughter, her father whistling as he buttered his toast.

All at once she felt like the radio show host, charged with jollying the caller along. 'So!' she said brightly. 'What's going on?'

'I just, well, I just wanted to check you were still coming?'

Jeannie looked up and caught sight of her face in the hall mirror. Her skin was now the colour of American-tan stockings, her eyes a frosted beige beneath heavily pencilled brows. The apples of her cheeks had been rouged a violent pink and her hair wreathed about in twists and twirls and loops. But it was her lips that bewildered her the most: the liner drawn beyond the natural limit of her mouth into an exaggerated bow, and then her mouth filled in with a glossy shade she recognised as Pink Heather.

'Jeannie?' Danny's voice hovered on the line.

'Yes,' she said. 'I'll be there.'

She watched the pink lips in the mirror shaping the

words. And as she watched, she had the odd sensation that it was not her, but someone else's mouth who had said them, and therefore should it transpire that she was not there at the station to meet him, well then, she could not be held responsible.

'Great!' He sounded relieved. 'Well, I'll see you there, on the platform, two o'clock.'

'Yep,' the lips said lightly. 'See you at two!'

And then she replaced the receiver and frowned at the strange young woman in the mirror.

Danny was sitting by the back door, polishing his shoes. It was still raining outside, and he was trying somehow to rewrite the narrative of their escape to accommodate the inclement weather. In his original plot, their departure had always been made on a clear, bright day, with a crisp blue sky and perhaps a light, encouraging breeze. He looked up at the window and saw nothing but flat, grey cloud.

'Grandad?' he called. 'Reckon this weather'll pick up this afternoon?'

His grandfather was drying dishes in the kitchen, and walked through carrying the tea towel and the rice pudding dish. 'I shouldn't think it likely,' he said, and ducked to look through the window. 'But the forecast's in the paper if you want to check.'

'Which paper?' Danny demanded.

His grandfather smirked. 'The one you've got covered in boot polish.'

Danny sighed and lifted his shoes. Sure enough, the weekend's weather report lay under a large black smudge. 'Bollocks,' he muttered. Perhaps it was a sign. Perhaps they should leave tomorrow instead.

'Have you got plans?' His grandfather was still standing in the doorway.

'I'm going to go away,' Danny said. 'Just for a couple of days or so, you know?' He tried his best to sound vague. He felt guilty about leaving his grandfather; they had fallen into a comfortable routine now, a steady pattern of cooking and cleaning and conversation.

'Would this be something to do with a lady-friend?' his grandfather asked.

Danny stared at the newspaper. Next to the weather report was an advert for a local butcher's shop, promising a week of special offers on mince and lamb chops. He trained his eyes firmly on the picture of the butcher, grinning broadly in his stripy apron.

'You've not got a girl in trouble again have you?'

Danny looked up sharply. 'No.' He shook his head. 'No, no. I just wanted us to go away, me and this girl, somewhere new, just, you know, see somewhere else.'

His grandfather carried on drying the dish, the glass squeaking under the rub of the towel. 'Here's my advice, son,' he said, without looking up. 'Now you're a bright lad, you've a brain, but you never stuck at learning, did you? You could've gone off to college, but instead you're working selling cups of tea at the railway station and talking about all these books you've read. And ever since you left your mum's you've been talking about where you're going to go next, if it's Paris or London or Dublin, thinking the next place you end up is going to solve all your problems.' He shook his head. 'Son, when I was your age, I had a profession, and I had a wife and a family. Real things. Things I had a responsibility to. Sooner or later, you have to decide where you're from and what you're doing and then you have stick to it. I'm not telling you not to go, I'm just telling you you're going to dream your life away if you're not careful.'

He paused, and let the tea towel drop to his side. 'I'll put the kettle on, shall I?'

Danny looked back to his shoes, let his eyes drift over the newspaper weather forecast, past the row of advertisements and across to the cluster of births, marriages, deaths, where one announcement caught his eye: 'Congratulations Jeannie and Jimmy on your wedding this Saturday!' it read, beneath an illustration of two wedding bells. 'With love from all the family.'

All spring the moths had been busy. Pressing their small amber bodies into darkened wardrobes and chests of drawers, quietly hiding their tiny eggs among the folds of fabric. With their gauzy wings and their filament legs they looked like wheat husks caught on jacket sleeves, snagged on cuffs, lapels, on hems. In a little while the larvae hatched and tucked in. They feasted on wool and on silk, they dined upon the carpet and the winter coats, burrowed among the woollens and the winter wear. In early May they found their way into the bag holding Jeannie's wedding dress, and lost themselves among the cream silk folds. And as they ate they left behind them a fine grey web and a trail of holes each no bigger than a pinprick.

When the bag was finally unzipped on that rainy June day, the damage was not immediately apparent. It was only once it hung on the wardrobe door, once Jeannie's mother had smoothed its skirt and flounced its netting, that she noticed some harm had befallen the dress. She picked up the hem and held it against her hand and saw that the pink of her fingers showed through several jagged holes.

'Oh no!' she cried. 'What a thing to happen!' It was hard not to see it as some kind of omen. She studied the rest of the dress, reassured herself that the worst of it was confined to the hem, and then she stood on the far side of the room and squinted; from this distance it might, she hoped, pass for cutwork.

Jeannie seemed curiously unruffled by the news. She picked up the skirt and ran her hand along it. 'Oh God!' she laughed. 'Poor Miss Crank!'

'It's not so bad …' Her mother tried to sound hearty. 'It looks sort of pretty, sort of lacy. I don't think anyone will notice, sweetheart.' A small, dun-coloured moth rose up then, out of the nets, and she clapped her hands together, squashed its soft, pale body between her palms.

It was too late, anyway, for anything to be done about it. That was the thing about a wedding day, Jeannie thought; it simply carried you along like a carnival queen.

'Breathe in!' Marie instructed, and hoicked at the corset strings. 'Bloody hell!' she gasped. 'I'm not sure I've got the brawn for this!'

Jeannie began to laugh, but it seemed laughing had become impossible within the confines of the corset. 'Remind me,' she said with a gulp, 'just why I'm doing this?'

'Oh now, Jeannie,' Marie said, knotting the strings tightly, 'it's because it is every new husband's dream to find his bride covered in corset-welts on their wedding night!'

'Ah yes,' Jeannie sighed, running her hands along the new curves of her waist. 'I knew there was a reason – and what a fine one it is!'

'You will find – and I speak from experience,' Marie dipped her voice, 'that corset-welts are the source of great marital bliss.'

Jeannie smiled. 'Is that your wise old married lady tip for me?' she asked.

'Hmm,' Marie pondered.

'You are happy, being married, aren't you?' Jeannie asked, a little panicked.

'Oh well, yes,' Marie said. 'Well, sometimes. I don't know, Jeans, mostly, yes.'

She was holding the dress now, ready for Jeannie to climb into. Jeannie hesitated, a nervous swimmer poised on the diving board.

'Mostly?' she asked. She was finding it difficult to breathe. Her ribs pushed against the bodice wall, but it stayed firm.

'Jeannie,' said Marie, plainly exasperated. 'You'll never find more than mostly.'

She shook the dress impatiently. Jeannie raised her arms above her head, closed her eyes and listened to Marie lifting the fabric over her head, a sweeping, rustling sound, like water. She held her breath and felt it slip over her outstretched arms until it dropped past her shoulders, and as it dropped she felt herself diving, deeper and deeper into the shadowy depths.

Jimmy was in the pub, nursing a pint of bitter. He pulled at his shirt collar. Mike, his best man, called across from the bar. 'A little drop of Dutch courage!' he announced. Jimmy shook his head and slowly sipped his beer. He hadn't touched sambuca since his stag do some weeks back, and even now it set his belly to pitching and swaying, took him back to that dark corner by the nightclub speakers where he had slumped, the bassline pumping through his head and his chest and his limbs, the room ebbing and flowing against him.

When they had finally found him, hauled him up and away across the dance floor towards the exit, he had been aware only of the sudden weight of his legs and the thin trail of saliva that strung from his lip to his chest. The next day his vomit had tasted of sambuca.

This morning he had awoken with a start. His head was thick with wine and the air was heavy with perfume. He had patted the bed beside him and was relieved to find it empty; Terri, he recalled, had finally left around ten o'clock, bundled into a taxi with a kiss and a promise that he would see her tomorrow. He knew then, as he knew now, that he had no intention of seeing her. She would be sitting in her lounge, waiting, wearing some natty little outfit, with her bags all packed up in the hall. And when he was late she would begin to worry. He pictured her rising from the sofa, her thigh muscles tensing as she stood, imagined the push of her calves as she crossed the carpet. She would stand at the window and look up the street. But it would be too late by then, the deal would be done, the sale would be made; he would be a married man, sitting in the back seat of a flash car with his bride, sailing through the streets to their reception.

He'd pulled on yesterday's pants and gone in search

of Alka Seltzer, turned on the radio as he passed; an advert for a bike shop in town spilled across the lounge, and then a Rod Stewart song he liked. He sang along as he searched through the kitchen drawers. 'Madame Onassis got nothin' on you!' he crooned, and plunked two tablets into a glass of water. The weather, he had noted, was miserable, but still Jimmy had felt a swell of sweet jubilation. It would, he decided, all be all right. At that precise moment, Mike had rung the doorbell. 'Get up, you fucker!' he called through the letterbox. 'You're getting married today!'

'C'mon, lad!' Mike told him now, and raised the shot glass. 'Get back on the horse!'

Jimmy sighed. He knew Mike well enough to know that it was easier just to down the shot and be done with it. He picked up the glass between finger and thumb and raised it to eye level. The liqueur stared placidly back at him. He drew it close to his mouth and a whiff of anise rushed to his nostrils. He braced himself, pressed the glass against his bottom lip and knocked it back.

What was a shot? Twenty-five millilitres? A pinch, nothing, a gulp. And yet it swilled around his mouth, a slow-moving, viscous pool of liquorice that covered his gums and clung to his teeth. Finally it oozed its way over the back of his tongue, past his wisdom teeth and down to his throat, where it whipped and burned and caused him to crumple his face and swallow and reach for his beer.

'Good lad!' Mike barked, and belted the table for good measure. The other drinkers stirred and looked up. This was a quiet pub, not far from the church, its only other customers a speckling of elderly men, undoubtedly regulars, and a dog that occasionally stood and lapped at a brown bowl set out by the fireplace, its heavy pink tongue making a satisfying plashing sound in the near silence of the bar.

The alcohol had begun to charge around Jimmy's body. His stomach burbled and his head swam, and he took a deep sip of beer to steady himself.

'How're you feeling?' Mike asked. 'Ready?'

For one terrified moment, Jimmy thought he was gearing up to another shot. He shook his head.

'No?' Mike raised his eyebrows. 'You should be, lad, it's been years coming, this!'

Jimmy realised that Mike meant the wedding. 'Oh,' he said. 'Right, that ...' But come to think of it, he wasn't entirely sure he was ready for that either.

'Last-minute doubts?' Mike pushed his shoulder. 'Unfinished business?' He looked around the pub. 'I'm sure we can find you one final fling before you say your vows.' His eyes fixed on the barmaid, a large woman in her mid-fifties wearing a cheap purple blouse, her hair dyed an uneven shade of auburn.

'Hey, gorgeous!' Mike called across to her. 'My mate's getting married today! Give him one last kiss as a free man will you, love?'

The barmaid looked over, rested one hand on the beer pump and the other on her broad hip. 'Getting married, eh?' She smiled. 'Well then!' She moved, measured out two more shots and carried them across to their table, swaying as she travelled across the room. She set them down near the empty glasses, licked a little spilled sambuca from her fingertip, and reached both arms across the table to cup Jimmy's face in her hands. Mike belted the table again and whistled through his teeth. 'Go on, Maggie!' rumbled one of the men from across the room.

Jimmy saw her face loom close, carrying with it the scent of talcum powder and stout and cheese and onion crisps. Her lips mushed heavily against his, propelled, it seemed, by the combined weight of her bosom and her belly and her hips. He counted the seconds: one, two, three, four, five ... And then she released him, flinging him back against the chair and rearing back upright with a jiggle. 'There you go, love!' she declared. 'Happy wedding day to you!' His mouth tasted of her lipstick, dusty and faintly cherry-scented.

When she was gone, carried on a wave of claps and cheers that made the small dog stand up and turn around, bewildered, Jimmy reached for the new shot glass, emptied the sambuca swiftly into his mouth, chasing away the taste of the kiss.

Mike laughed. 'Now you're ready to get married!' he said warmly and knocked back his shot.

'I shagged Terri.' Jimmy blurted out the words, as if commanded by the alcohol now cantering through his veins.

Mike looked at him, stunned. 'When?'

'The last few months.' Whether or not the confession had been a good idea still hung in the balance, weighted on one side by the relief of having told someone, and on the other by a dark and oily fear.

'More than once?' Mike asked.

How to tell him, Jimmy wondered, of the afternoons, the evenings, the mornings even, spent wound up in Terri's sheets, the wine, the takeaways, the cigarettes shared in bed, the strange kind of peace he had felt staring up at her ceiling as she slept, listening to the brush of distant traffic, the world rushing by far away from this warm, safe place.

'Yes,' was all he answered mutely.

'Is it over?'

Jimmy thought of the finality of last night, of the line he seemed to draw between them as she climbed into the minicab, of the sense of resolution he felt as he locked the door and listened to the car make its way up the street, to the junction and far away.

He looked at Mike and nodded. 'Yes,' he said.

Mike sipped his beer a little sternly, shuffled his neck in his stiff shirt collar. 'Well then, under the circumstances,' he said, 'I think we'd best keep this little secret between you and me and no further. Don't go telling Jeannie, whatever you do.'

It seemed to Mike, and he spoke from experience, that any man who confessed to an affair did so because he wanted relief from his own guilt. He wanted to be forgiven, to be told it was all OK. It was, he believed, one more selfish act on top of another selfish act, pushing your own need for absolution before the feelings of your wife. No, the thing to do – the right, upstanding thing to do, was to live with what you had done, to live with the guilt; that was your punishment for your crime.

He looked at Jimmy. 'All right,' he said. 'It stays between us, and here's your penance – four Hail Marys and another shot of sambuca.'

He stood up and strode to the bar. Left alone, Jimmy pressed his face into his hands and breathed a long, liquoricey sigh of relief.

Jeannie wished she could make it stop, just a pause even, just for a moment stand by herself and catch her breath. But instead the day seemed to have acquired a momentum of its own; it bore her aloft, onwards to the church, before she even knew she was ready, before she even knew she was dressed and dolled up and made into a bride, she was spilling out of the house and on to the drive and someone was taking pictures, and Dannielle was picking up the moth-eaten train of her dress lest it drag in the puddles that pooled in the gravel.

She was in the car now. The door was shut and she was steadying herself amid the damp, warm air that smelled of old leather seating and her father's cologne. In front of her she could see the back of the driver's head. He was wearing a funny formal cap, beneath which ran a curve of oily black hair. On the top of his right ear there was a slick of what was probably gel or wax or pomade. She looked over at her father, and he squeezed her hand. 'I can't believe my little girl is getting married,' he said, as if he had been rehearsing the line after hearing it on a television show somewhere.

'Oh, I'm a big girl now,' she answered, and smiled, and was then hit by a jolt of nausea. She wound down the window just a touch, and the breeze carried in a flurry of spittle that fell lightly on her face and her shoulder and her white nylon veil.

Onwards the day charged. The streets sailed by too quickly, the houses she had known all her life blurring past as if they meant nothing. There was her primary school, and the library, the stop where she caught the school bus, the corner shop where she had first bought cigarettes, her grandmother's house, Marie's. There in the beauty salon she saw the customers lined up before the mirrors and the stylists milling about and waving their hands and picking up hairdryers and laughing.

Everyone they passed seemed to look up and point. Little girls in raincoats waved, grandmothers at bus stops watched and smiled, cars travelling in the opposite direction slowed down and tooted their horns. Such was the effect of a wedding car, sailing through rain-greased streets beneath a pale June sky, a happy blur of cream paint and pink ribbon rippling in the wind, that it somehow served to take the place of the sun this grey afternoon.

'How are you feeling?' her father asked. She turned to look at him: his face was jowelling now, but had once been as comely as Dannielle's, and though his hair was fading and thinning at the crown, and lines had run across his forehead, splayed across his temples and around the corners of his mouth, his eyes were still a soft, encouraging brown. She did not answer but met his gaze and gripped his fingers and smiled.

How was she feeling? She closed her eyes and thought. She felt like a mote of dust, a tiny speck, falling through some vast and cavernous space. She was turning and tumbling and twisting, and as she turned, sometimes she felt the light fall upon her, and then everything seemed clear and bright. And at others she was in darkness, and she felt herself indecipherable and darkened and lost. And though she danced and dallied and floated through the air, she was gripped by the knowledge that gravity pulled her inexorably downwards, down towards the church, towards the long cool aisle and the altar, to where she would finally stop, and stand and be still.

She opened her eyes and saw that they had reached the edge of town: the discount stationery store, the fireplace shop, the florist, the Christian bookshop, the Seven Stars. The car paused on Station Road, the Saturday traffic growing heavier as they neared the town centre. Ahead of them sat the 639 bus, and on the back seat were three teenage girls, giggling on their way to the shops, young and free and happy.

The car crawled forward, making a slow, painful advance beneath the railway bridge. Jeannie stared down at her bouquet, at the pale pink roses and the bursts of gypsophila, the fronds of dark green leaves. She pressed it up to her face, so she could breathe in the heavy rose scent, and she thought again of her grandmother's garden, of the perfume she made in jam-jars, and the sound of the blackbird, singing out into the evening air.

When she looked up they were in front of the station. The automatic doors were opening and shutting, and a man in an orange tabard brushed the pavement. She watched the taxi cabs drawing up outside, the people spilling out with their bags and their suitcases, kissing their loved ones goodbye, leaving lipstick on cheeks and perfume on jackets, running through their doors, hoping to make their trains.

'Wait!' she said, and grabbed at the door handle. The

driver looked up at the rear-view mirror, his eyes darting towards the peak of his smart little cap. The door was open now, the wet air gusting against the ivory fabric of her dress. The driver braked. She looked at her father. 'I just have to ...' she poked one leg out of the door, pressed her foot against the puddled tarmac, so the water rose darkly up the cream satin toe. 'I won't be a minute,' she said, and ducked out into the rain.

She saw the heads turn, strain to look back at the bride running across the road, darting through the traffic and the crowds and the drizzle. Her shoes pinched her toes, rubbed her heel, their soles slipped as she hurried through the automatic doors and on to the smooth floor of the ticket office. It was only at this moment, as the line of travellers before the ticket window turned and gawped and nudged each other and stifled their laughter and began to talk in animated whispers, that Jeannie realised she had no idea what she was doing.

She could not very well head to the platform, pitter-patter up the steps with her bridal train bunched in her hand and her veil billowing out behind her. She could not slide into a buffet window seat, take Danny's freckled hand and kiss his palm. Yet she had an overwhelming desire to go back to the beginning, to start again and set things right. She looked at the line of scandalised ticket-buyers, she looked up at the monitors, and then she pushed her way into the ladies' toilets.

It was just the same. The yellowy light, the whirl of paper towels, the scent of urine and bleach. Jeannie headed into one of the cubicles, awkwardly manoeuvred herself around, hitched up her wedding dress and sat down on the cold damp seat. She felt calm, one cream satin foot on the door, reading the familiar graffiti. Her mind seemed to still, the dust seemed to settle, and she stood up, smoothed down her dress, pulled the chain.

It was an afterthought, really. An idea that came to her as she lathered her hands, rinsed and towelled them dry. She looked at the scratched square of mirror, at the tired old scrawl about Shelley. She reached into the cream satin bag on her wrist and drew out her lipstick, still pristine and pointed in the tube. She reached across the basin, pressed the hard pink tip against the mirror and wrote the words JEANNIE + DANNY in block print, then circled it with a heart.

'It's fine,' she said, as she climbed back into the car and met the worried brown eyes of her father. She felt bolder now, as if she had tied up a loose end, and as the driver pulled away towards the town, she watched the shopfronts stream by, smiled back at the faces as they passed.

The rain had grown heavier by the time they reached the church. It fell on the footpath and dotted the headstones in the churchyard, it pelted the roses and the ribbon tied to the iron arch above the gate. Jeannie climbed out of the car, ducked away from the umbrella in the driver's hand, felt the rain speckle her face, run through the heavy make-up and the tumbles and twists of her hair. There was, she noticed, still confetti gathered in the gutter from yesterday's wedding, bobbing about a little now, beginning a multicoloured stream of bells and horseshoes and hearts and clovers all down the hill.

Father Michael stood in the doorway, his face still pale and inscrutable, his eyes just as milky. 'Are you ready?' he asked.

From inside she heard the huffing of the church organ, the shuffling of bodies as they turned around to see the bride. Jeannie nodded, and with a pat on the shoulder he sent Dannielle and Marie sailing towards the altar.

She pulled her veil down gently over her face, and her father linked his arm into hers, the heavy serge of his suit pressing against her skin. Dimly, through the nylon netting, she could make out Jimmy, standing like a distant destination at the end of the aisle. She breathed deeply, filled her lungs with the soft church air. There was a swell of noise, of people rising in the pews and the organ beginning, and in her mind it became the sound of an engine, of a train preparing to leave the station.

It was a familiar feeling, though it took her a moment to place it. She walked the length of the aisle, catching glimpses of the pews: the hymn-sheets stacked up, and the cushions for prayer, the handbags and shawls and wedding gifts, all the faces, muted by her veil, staring out at her as she passed. And when she reached the end, she looked up at Jimmy and at Father Michael, she stood at the altar and she felt as if she were back at the station, on the pale concrete promontory jutting out between the lines, where the wind jostled her hair and rain spat in her eyes. She waited to hear the whistle, but instead came Father Michael's voice, clearing his throat with a high, brisk cough, his words pushing towards her, gathering speed, rushing by in a blur of grey.

ACKNOWLEDGEMENTS

Thank you to Jon Riley, Charlotte Clerk and Peter Straus, for all their hard work, and for bearing with me.

To my parents, Nick, Paul, Dolly, Amy, Joe, Alice, Tom, Cecilia and Janis, for always putting up with me.

To Oliver Gibson, Michael Hann, Ian Rickson and Gil Vernon, for encouraging me along the way.